The Obsidian Lounge Episodes 1-5

The Obsidian Lounge

Jasmine Bishop

Published by Heartness Crane Publishing, 2022.

This is a work of fiction. Similarities to real people, places, or events are entirely coincidental.

THE OBSIDIAN LOUNGE EPISODES 1-5

First edition. September 22, 2022.

Copyright © 2022 Jasmine Bishop.

ISBN: 979-8215751107

Written by Jasmine Bishop.

Amanda glared at the digital clock on her nightstand. Six in the morning. She'd woken up too early again, hot and irritated, like she had every day this week.

I'm sick of this.

She got up, brushed her teeth, and grabbed a glass of water from the kitchen. Then she lay back in bed, paralyzed, dreading the thought of another night of waiting tables.

If I start coffee now, I won't get back to sleep. Why is this happening?

She tossed the sheet on the floor in frustration. Her blinds were closed, but she already sensed the hot, bright sun lurking outside. She sighed and turned the box fan she'd bought at Fred Meyer last week all the way up, then flopped back on the bed.

Cool air washed over her. She wiped the sweat off her forehead with her hand and wiped it on the underwear she'd worn to bed last night. Her whole body was sweaty, her shirt and underwear soaked through. Her shirt clung to her. Irritated, she took it off and let it join the sheet on the floor. She looked down at her sweaty breasts and wiped them off with her palms. Instantly, a nipple perked up.

Well, here we go. Hello, there.

She took the nipple between her fingers and gave it a slow twist, savoring the pleasure, then licked her palm and slid it smoothly across her breast. She moved her other hand down to explore herself. Her pussy was slick with sweat, and she stroked the outside of her panties before guiding her hand underneath. With two fingers she opened herself, making soft circles around her clit.

If I have to be awake now, I might as well make the most of it.

She slid her panties off and pushed them away as she continued to stroke herself and a lazy smile grew on her face.

"Order up!"

The bell in the window rang out again, loud and impatient. Amanda had worked at Sam's Clubhouse for less than a week, but she already loathed it.

"Be right there," she called over her shoulder. "Hold on." She rushed to drop a couple of burgers off at table seven, reminding herself that table twelve still needed water and the couple at two had asked for soda refills.

"Order up," the cook repeated. Amanda ignored him, dropped the plates off, and rushed back.

"I'm dying out there," she said. "I don't know where Louise ran off to, but I need help."

The cook wiped his forehead with a hairy arm and scowled. His face was flushed, and he looked like he was going to have a heart attack at any moment. "Oh yeah? I need help, too, sister." He pointed at the chicken fried steak dinner in the window. "That food's getting cold up there and there's no way I'm making it again. Just move that cute ass of yours a little faster."

Amanda sighed and grabbed the plate out of the window.

This is such bullshit. I can't keep working these jobs. I'm so fucking sick of restaurants.

She dropped the plate off in front of a single gentleman sitting at the counter. "Can I get you anything else?" she asked.

The man peered dimly from behind his baseball cap. "Steak sauce."

On a chicken fried steak? Disgusting. But you do you, buddy.

"Absolutely." She reached under the counter and set the bottle in front of him. "There you go."

"Thanks, sweetie."

Ugh. The shit I put up with.

"Of course." Amanda gathered all her strength to summon a smile. "Let me know if you need anything else."

She spotted Louise on her way back to the hostess station.

"There you are," she said. "I've been looking for you. They need water on twelve and soda refills on two."

Louise rolled her eyes as she ambled over to the soda fountain. Amanda dropped the plate off, picked up the empty glasses on two, and speed-walked over.

"Where have you been?"

"I was in the bathroom."

Louise was young, nineteen or twenty, and had proven to be a pain in the ass every night this week.

You're cute, girl, but your attitude sucks. Good looks can only get you so far.

"Look, do you mind helping me in a bit? There are a lot of tables to clear, and I'm really behind." She flipped through her pad and organized her tickets. "I can't believe this place doesn't have a busser."

"I don't think so," Louise told her.

"Excuse me?"

Louise met her gaze. "I'm the hostess. I seat people and bring them menus and water. Sometimes I answer the phone. I don't bus tables. That's your job."

"Really?"

"Really." Louise placed her hand on her hip, defiantly. "And you'd better not skimp me on my tips. You new girls always try that. I get twenty percent."

"Susan told me you get ten percent."

Louise scoffed. "Well, someone misinformed you. I get twenty percent, and that's before you tip the kitchen out."

Amanda stormed off. She looked at the old, dingy clock on the wall, clouded with years of nicotine stains from when you could still smoke inside. It was seven o'clock.

Just another hour. I can do this.

Amanda stayed a half hour late refilling the sugars and salt and pepper shakers and missed the eight o'clock bus, like she knew she would. The next one didn't come for an hour, and she resigned herself to a long wait. She sat on the bench in the bus shelter as the wind whipped rain inside. By the time the bus arrived, the legs of her pants were soaked through and she was shivering.

After a five-minute walk in the rain, she made it back to the small two-bedroom apartment she shared with her friend Diane. She stripped off her black and white work clothes and threw them on top of the hamper, then took a hot shower and changed into her favorite blue bathrobe. She brushed her long, dark hair and padded out to the kitchen.

She was crouched in front of the fridge with the door open when Diane came home holding a pizza box.

"Hey, you. Hungry?" Diane asked.

Amanda looked up at her and beamed. "You're an angel."

Diane set the box on the counter. She took off her watch cap and revealed a mess of blond hair. "Just leftovers from some stupid work party. Veggie, of course. All yours if you want it."

Amanda reached in, pulled out a couple of slices, and put them on a plate. "This is perfect."

Diane set her purse on the counter and hung her coat on the rack. "Still hate the new job?" she asked.

"It's the worst."

"That bad?"

"I don't know if I'll make it another week. Everyone is so terrible there." She took a bite of cold pizza. "And if that cook makes one more smart comment about my ass, I swear I'm walking out."

"Your ass? What did he say?"

"That it was cute. And that I should move it faster."

"Well, he's not wrong."

"That I should move it?" Amanda gave a little shake of her tail. The food gave her energy, and she could feel her strength returning.

"That it's cute."

Amanda blushed. She'd been getting hints that Diane was interested in her lately. It hadn't been obvious when they were friends in college, but ever since they'd graduated and moved in together things had been different.

Diane took off her sweater, a faded Metallica t-shirt clinging to her chest, and Amanda's eyes strayed. Diane rarely wore a bra. Her breasts might have been small, but her nipples poked out provocatively.

Hey, maybe I'm interested, too. It could be fun to play around a little. I still can't believe we never have.

Diane moved to the couch and unlaced her black Doc Martens. Her legs were spread, and Amanda glimpsed the ripped black leggings under her bleached denim skirt.

She does have great legs.

Diane dropped her boots in the corner and walked to the kitchen. "It's a wine night. You with me?"

Amanda nodded. "Definitely. Let the wine flow freely."

Diane handed her a glass, and their fingers touched for an instant. A soft brush, a ripple of energy.

She looks tough on the outside, but I know how soft she really is.

"You look so comfy in your robe, I think I'll join you," Diane said. "You want to watch a show or something?"

"I'll be right here," Amanda said. "I'm not moving for anything." She set her wine on the coffee table and reached for a second piece of pizza.

The next day at Sam's wasn't as bad. Amanda had found her groove and was becoming more confident. It was still a grind, though. The customers were rude, and the day server had left as soon as Amanda clocked in without doing any of her side work.

Toward the end of the night, a woman walked in by herself. She appeared to be in her early forties, immaculately clothed in a black dress. Her dark hair was concealed by a black, wide-brimmed hat, and she wore a silver necklace which drew attention to her full, round breasts. Amanda could tell she wasn't a typical Sam's customer. Louise gave her one of the booths by the windows.

Amanda grabbed her order pad and approached the woman in awe. "Welcome to Sam's Clubhouse," she said. "Would you like to hear about our today's specials?"

The menu sat on the table, untouched. Amanda's heart beat hard in her chest, the palms of her hands inexplicably damp.

This lady is truly gorgeous.

"Just tea, please. Earl Grey, if you have it."

"Absolutely. Would you like cream?"

"Yes, that would be lovely." The woman handed the menu back, and their fingers touched. An instant spark of connection. The woman met her eyes with an invitation to look longer. They maintained eye contact for a moment, then Amanda took the menu and hurried back to the hostess station.

"Let me guess, nothing to eat," Louise said.

"That's right."

"Earl Grey tea?"

Amanda turned to her. "How did you know?"

"Miss Trent comes here about once a month. Usually around an hour before close. Sits in the same booth every time, and never gets anything to eat. She just orders tea and hangs out for a while. Sometimes she writes in her journal." Louise half-heartedly rubbed a damp rag on the counter, smearing the grease around in a half-circle.

Amanda filled a cup with boiling water and grabbed a package of tea from the boxes stacked on the counter.

"Suck up to her," Louise said. "She's a good tipper."

Amanda set the tea-bag and cup of boiling water on a saucer, grabbed a dish of creamers, and walked over.

"I've never seen you here before," Miss Trent said. "Did you just start?"

"Yes, this is my first week."

"And how do you like Sam's so far?"

"It's fine."

"Really?"

For some reason, Amanda felt compelled to tell her the truth. "No." She breathed a sigh of relief, as if a weight had been lifted from her chest. "Honestly, I can't stand it here."

"That's more like it." Miss Trent opened a creamer and poured it into her tea.

Amanda took a deep breath. "Wow. It felt so good to say that out loud. I do, I hate waitressing."

"Then why are you a waitress?" Miss Trent added a small amount of sugar to her cup, stirred it, and set the spoon on her napkin.

Amanda sighed. "I don't know have a lot of options. A lot of college graduates can't find work in their fields right now."

"That might be true, but there's no reason to limit yourself. There are a lot of things you can do. You just need to be open to possibilities. You have an exceptional mind, I can tell." The woman held her hand out. "My name is Erica Trent."

Amanda took her hand. Erica's grasp was firm but comforting. "Amanda. Amanda Jones."

"It's a pleasure to meet you, Amanda. I've been coming here for years, and you're the most charming server I've ever had. I hope we can become friends."

So do I, Erica Trent.

"I have to go check on my other tables," Amanda said. "Let me know if you need anything else."

"Of course you do. I'm fine with my tea for the moment. Thank you."

Amanda sighed in frustration when she saw all the empty, dirty tables left over from the dinner rush. She got to work filling bus tubs and hauling them to the dishwasher, wiping the tables down and replacing the silverware. Ten minutes of work and the dining room was mostly clear, only a few tables left. She walked over to check on Miss Trent.

"How is your tea? Do you need a warm-up?"

"No, thank you. I need to leave soon. I have one errand to run before I go home."

"All right. I can bring the check anytime but can tell you right now it's two dollars for the tea."

"Let me take care of it now." Erica reached in her billfold and brought out a ten-dollar bill. "You keep it, for being so kind this evening."

Erica held the bill out to her, and Amanda noticed her hands again. Soft and aristocratic, a woman of nobility.

Amanda took the bill and stuck it in her apron. "Thank you, that's very kind." She turned away, walked to a dirty table and began filling another bus tub.

A few minutes after Erica left, a couple walked in. Louise handed them menus and sat them in a booth.

Great. Twenty minutes until close. Thanks a lot.

Just as she had expected, the last table stayed way past close. Even after she'd turned off the neon sign in the window, asked them pointedly if they'd like anything else this evening, and set the bill in front of the man's nose, they sat there, oblivious. And, of course, she missed the bus again.

As she resigned herself to a thirty-minute wait in the freezing rain, a black Mercedes SUV pulled up to the bus stop and flashed its lights. Amanda looked up and recognized Erica sitting in the back.

The rear passenger window slid down, and Erica called out to her. "Oh, dear. You're soaked. Are you going home? Would you like a ride?"

Amanda grabbed her purse and stood up. "Which way are you going?"

"Where do you live?"

"I'm off Barbur, near Burlingame Fred Meyer."

"Come inside and get out of the rain."

A handsome young man in a chauffeur's uniform bounded out of the driver's seat. He was clean-shaven, his short brown hair under a cap, his wide smile genuine. He walked around the car, tipped his hat for Amanda, and opened the back door, welcoming her inside.

"Allow me to introduce my driver, Lawrence," Erica said.

Amanda smiled at Lawrence and gratefully entered the car. She had never ridden in a vehicle this nice before. The back seat was large and roomy, the seats soft. "Thank you. I was going to be sitting out there a while."

Erica had taken her hat off, and Amanda marveled at her thick, black hair. "I don't know how people can take public transportation every day. I had to take it once years ago. Let me tell you, never again."

The SUV had an amazing sound system, with speakers on the roof and along the tops of the doors. She recognized the music as an old Cure song, one of her favorites.

Well, she has great taste in music. Great taste in a lot of things, it would appear.

Amanda settled in and felt a pleasant warmness on her bottom.

"Please let Lawrence know if the seat warmer is too much for you," Erica said. "I never use it myself."

"It's wonderful." Just a few minutes ago she'd been sitting in the cold, grimly determined to wait for a dirty bus full of creepers and drunks. Now she had been transported to a new reality - warm, dry, and luxurious.

"It's fabulous," she said. "I've never had one of these before."

"It's good to be open to new experiences. Wouldn't you agree, Amanda?"

"Oh, definitely."

Lawrence drove swiftly and assuredly, navigating the winding road out of downtown. stopping at each red light with ease and precision.

"Tell Lawrence where you live. He can take you right to your door," Erica said. "He knows this town so well, Amanda. I'd be absolutely lost without him."

Amanda gave Lawrence directions, and he took his hand off the wheel for one moment to give her a thumbs up. "I'll get you home, Miss Amanda."

"This world is full of amazing treasures. All you have to do is ask for them. Or take them for yourself." Erica laughed. "I've thought about your situation, Amanda. You told me you're not happy in your current position."

"I mean, I'm just doing it to pay the bills until something else comes along."

"I said earlier that I can tell you have an exceptional mind. You should use it to your advantage." Erica leaned in, as if to tell her a secret. "I don't believe I told you what I do for a living."

"No, you didn't."

"I'm a ghostwriter."

"You write books for people?"

"Basically, yes. I give people with more money than literary talent a way to tell their stories. Of course, I'll never be famous, and that's just fine with me." Erica laughed. "I've become quite sought after and find myself in need of a research assistant."

Amanda looked at her, surprised.

She is not offering me a job. Is she?

"Dictation, research, transcribing notes. These things are all quite time-consuming. I'm not able to do them all myself. I have an extensive project coming up, my biggest yet, and I need someone to help me." Erica smiled. "I pay extremely well. More than you make at Sam's Clubhouse, I can guarantee that."

"Why me?"

"I can tell we would work well together. You're bright, and I have no doubt you could do the work. I want to give this opportunity to someone who will appreciate it." Erica stretched back, her skirt tightening around her thighs and creeping upward. Amanda caught a quick glimpse, then turned her head.

I'd better not let her catch me doing that.

Lawrence turned on to her street, and Erica took a business card out of her purse and handed it to her. "Please think about it and let me know what you decide. No pressure, but I need an answer soon, otherwise I'll have to call the temp agency. And I'd rather not do that. They're so impersonal, wouldn't you agree?"

Amanda nodded and put the card in her purse. "I'll let you know. Thanks for the ride." She waved to Lawrence. "Thank you, Lawrence. You were wonderful."

Lawrence got out of the car, walked around, and opened the door for her. As she grabbed her purse, he tipped his hat. "It was a pleasure, Miss Amanda. I hope to see you again soon."

"Have a good night, Amanda," Erica called to her.

"I'll call you."

Erica laughed. "I expect it."

The car drove off into the night and Amanda walked up the steps to her apartment.

What is happening? Why does this woman turn me on so much?

It was magnetism, a strong sexual connection. A switch had turned on in her body, and she there was only one way to turn it off. She needed release.

Diane was on the couch in pajamas and the same threadbare Metallica t-shirt she'd worn yesterday. She was watching an old horror movie, a half-empty bottle of merlot on the kitchen counter.

Amanda took her coat off and hung it up.

"You're home early," Diane said.

"I got a ride. It's a really cool story."

"Good, I was afraid you walked out." Diane asked.

"Not tonight," Amanda said. "It actually wasn't so bad."

Amanda sat down on the couch and took her shoes off. "I've got to get out of these pants," she said. "They're so tight." She unbuttoned her shirt as she walked to her bedroom, then turned around, her bra exposed. "Are you going to stay up for a while?"

"Sure."

"Great. Don't go anywhere."

Amanda threw her white work shirt in the hamper and took off her pants. She searched her dresser for the sexiest lingerie she owned - a black, lacy piece that went down to the middle of her thighs - and set it on the bed. She'd worn it exactly once before it had gone to live in the bottom drawer with her vibrators and the rest of her collection of toys.

The shower was wonderful. A knot had formed above her right shoulder, and she felt the strain in her arms from carrying plates back and forth.

Yes, I'm definitely calling Erica tomorrow.

She poured lavender body wash on a scrubby, rubbed her stomach until it foamed, and appraised her body. Her knees were too bony, her breasts too small. There was that weird birthmark above her hip.

She watched the soap bubbles stream down her legs, past her dark pubic hair. She liked how a little hair looked. Nothing too wild, just enough for a little mystery.

She took the detachable showerhead off and washed her legs and feet, then her thighs. She rubbed the inside of her thighs, and bells went off.

That's good.

She kept stroking, bringing the shower head up so the water streamed on her pussy. She took one of her breasts in her other hand and pinched her nipple, which was already hard. Reaching down, she stroked herself with two fingers. Her lips gently parted and her little bud rose.

Amanda was a frequent and unashamed masturbator and could finish herself in a few minutes if her mind was right. She quickly brought herself to the brink of an orgasm.

Cool down. Save the first one for Diane.

She moved her hand away and turned the water off.

Amanda dried herself and slipped into the lingerie. When she walked back out to the living room, Diane was where she'd left

her, watching the same movie. Amanda swung by the kitchen for a glass of wine and sat down next to her on the couch.

"Well, look at you," Diane said. "Very sexy. What's the occasion?"

"You don't think it's too much?"

"Are you kidding? You're hot. My only question is why you don't wear it all the time?"

"I kind of forgot I had it. It's been sitting in a drawer for years."

"Well, that's a waste."

Amanda took a sip of wine.

If I can hold out a little longer, I can blame it on the wine. But what if things get weird?

Diane looked over at her, a gleam of mischief in her eye. "It looks comfortable."

"Do you want to feel?"

"Sure." Diane held her hand out and touched the silky material. It had been so long since anyone had touched her, and she shivered with anticipation. She took Diane's hand in hers and ran it down her chest. It cupped her breast and grazed her nipple, which was hard again. Diane spontaneously made a circle around it with her finger, and that's all it took.

She grabbed Diane's hips and brought her in for a kiss. Their lips met, and she rolled her tongue across Diane's.

Diane pulled away. "Amanda-"

"Shh. I want this."

She leaned in and held Diane while they kissed. She slowly slid down until her knees were on the carpet and grabbed Diane's ass with both hands. Taking a deep breath, she softly kissed the outside of her thin cotton lounge pants. Diane raised

herself up from the couch and Amanda buried her mouth deeper into her.

Diane pulled her pants down, leaving just her black panties on. Amanda gave her thighs a few soft nibbles. "You really know your way down there," Diane said.

"I've had some experience."

"We should have spent more time together in college. We could have had some fun."

"We're having fun now," Amanda said, sliding her hand down Diane's panties.

Diane moaned softly in anticipation. "I've waited so long for this," she said. "You know that, right?"

"It will be worth the wait. I promise." She took Diane's panties off in one motion and tossed them next to the couch. Diane's pubic hair was trimmed, a soft, blond mound, tempting and fragrant. Amanda lapped at her, savoring the scent.

"You smell so good." She went straight to her clit, tonguing Diane's lips open until they spread wide and she found what she was looking for. Continuing to press Diane's ass, she went deeper and the circles she made with her tongue went faster. Diane moaned again, spreading her legs wide.

"I like this side of you, Amanda," Diane said. "I could get used to this."

Amanda's tongue twirled harder. Diane's body tensed, and Amanda powered through until Diane was shivering and gasping and her juice covered Amanda's mouth.

Diane got up from the couch and picked Amanda off the floor. "Come to the bedroom," she said. "It's your turn now."

In the bedroom, Diane tore Amanda's lingerie off and threw her down on the bed. She went right for Amanda's wet pussy. She licked her fingers and reached for Amanda's nipples, making circles with her fingers while she got to work going down on her.

We could have been doing this the whole time. Well, better late than never.

Diane grabbed Amanda's ass with both hands and thrust her tongue against Amanda's throbbing clit. The pressure was intense and built up quickly. It didn't take her long to come, an explosive orgasm that sent waves of pleasure through her body.

Diane got up and walked to the dresser. "What about this?" she asked, reaching into a top drawer. She brought out a small pink vibrator. Picking up a small tube of lubricant from her bedside table, she handed them both to Amanda. "Use it on me?"

Amanda twisted the knob and watched it come alive. It whirred softly, and she laughed. "This little thing works for you?"

"Hey, it might not look like much, but it gets the job done. You got something better?"

Amanda laughed again. "I'll show you my arsenal sometime."

"I'm game anytime you want."

Amanda uncapped the jar, took some in her fingers, and traced around Diane's labia. The vibe slid right in. She gave a few tentative strokes, steadily going deeper. She guided it up to her clit and smiled as Diane moaned with delight.

Moving around, she kissed Diane on the mouth, her right hand controlling the vibe. Diane arched her back and Amanda thrust the vibe in deeper, sliding it in and out. She took one of Diane's breasts in her mouth and sucked on her hard nipple. Diane shook with the intensity of her orgasm and collapsed on the bed.

"You're amazing," Diane said.

"You're pretty good yourself," Amanda replied.

Diane had left for work when Amanda woke to the sound of her alarm the next morning.

At least I slept through the night for a change. That's an improvement.

She felt better than she had in a long time. As she walked to the kitchen to start coffee, she saw a note on the counter.

"Last night was great! Let's do it again soon. D."

As she waited for coffee to brew, she looked around the apartment. It was basic, a Sears catalog come to life. The furniture was cheap, and neither one of them had an eye for decoration. She might have lived there, but Amanda had never thought of it as her home.

She made a simple breakfast of scrambled eggs and toast with strawberry jam. She turned on the news while she ate but didn't pay any attention to it.

The couple on table six had been a headache from the time they walked in. When the woman sent her toast back for the second time, Amanda got a little snippy with them.

"I want to speak to your manager," the woman said.

"Fine." She walked back to the office and found Susan playing solitaire on her phone, which was all Amanda had seen her do in the week she'd been there.

"There's a customer out there asking for you," she said.

Susan sighed and looked up from her phone. "What now?"

"They've been complaining ever since they walked in," Amanda said. "Please come out here and calm them down. I have orders in the window."

Susan sighed, put her phone in her pocket, and followed her out to the floor.

"I'm the manager," Susan said as she approached the table. "How can I help you?"

Amanda stood behind her and watched as the orders piled up in the window. The bell rang over and over.

The woman torn into Susan immediately. "This girl can't get a simple order of toast right. First, it's not toasted enough. I send it back and it's burned. What are you going to do about this?"

"I'm doing everything I can to make this right," Amanda explained. "I can't control what comes out of the kitchen, but I will talk to the cook again. I'll fix it."

Susan glared at her and turned to the woman. "I apologize about this, ma'am," she said. "We'll make this right. Won't we, Amanda?"

"Yes. That's what I'm telling you. I'll take the toast back. I'll talk to the cook. I'll make it right."

The woman exploded. "You said that ten minutes ago. Still no toast. Where is my toast?"

"You're fucking unbelievable, lady." Amanda didn't know where the words came from. They just came out.

"What did you say?"

Amanda paused for a moment, then a delicious feeling of liberation came over her and she turned to Susan. "I don't get paid enough to put up with this shit," she said as she untied her apron and threw it on the floor. Her order pad fell out of the pocket and the pen rolled under a table. She walked over and grabbed her purse and coat from under the register.

"You're fired," Susan called after her.

"You can't fire me if I quit," Amanda said. She walked out of Sam's Clubhouse into the bright, sunny afternoon. A light breeze blew through her hair, refreshing her as she waited patiently for the walk signal to turn green.

Home again, Amanda picked the business card off her dresser and held it between her fingers. It was an elegant card, printed on thick, expensive-looking stock. **Erica Trent - Author Services** was written in bold, black script, and underneath was an email address and phone number. She dialed the number and a female voice answered. "Trent residence."

"Hello. May I speak to Miss Trent, please?"

"May I ask what this is regarding?" The voice had an edge of impatience to it.

"My name is Amanda Jones. I met Miss Trent last night. She asked me to call."

"Well, Miss Trent is not available right now."

"Oh."

There was silence on the other end of the line. "However," the voice finally continued, "she has been expecting your call and would like to invite you to dinner at Trent Manor tonight. Are you available?"

Well, I don't have a job to go to anymore. Yes, I'm available.

"Sure. I mean, yes."

"You're going to need directions. If you're taking I-5 North, take Exit 47. Drive ten miles-"

"I'm sorry," Amanda interrupted, "I don't drive."

"You don't have a car?"

Amanda sighed. "No. Let me see if I can see if I can get a ride from my housemate."

"Don't bother. I'll send Lawrence to get you. Does he have your address?"

Amanda told her the address. "This is very kind of you."

"You seem to have made quite an impression on Miss Trent, Amanda. Expect Lawrence at eight o'clock sharp."

"Thank you so much," Amanda began, but she was talking to dead air. The call was over.

Diane got home around seven, carrying the mail and a bag of groceries. She set them on the counter and her face brightened when she saw Amanda in the living room.

"What are you doing home early?" she asked.

Amanda couldn't hide her smile. "Oh, you know. Not busting my ass at that greasy spoon anymore." She stood up and twirled around in excitement. "Guess who quit her job today?"

Diane rushed over and embraced her. "Oh, Amanda, you did it. You really did it. I'm so happy for you."

She inhaled Diane's scent, and memories of last night flooded her mind. Going down on her had been so hot. And, of course, the vibrator.

That dinky little thing. She really needs something better. I could pick one out that would blow her mind.

"Thanks, babe." Amanda gave her a quick kiss on the cheek.

"That place must have been really bad."

"Oh, it was. The worst yet. You should have seen their faces when I walked. It was so great."

"You just walked out?"

"Sure did."

"Good for you. You don't need that kind of stress." Diane poured a glass of merlot from the bottle on the counter. "Of course, there's still rent. And the electric bill just came today." She pointed to the envelope on the counter. "Were you able to put anything away in savings?"

"That's the best part," Amanda said. "I already have another job lined up."

"Really? That was fast. Where are you working?" She paused. "Don't tell me it's another restaurant."

"No, thank God. This woman came into Sam's last night and she wants to hire me as her assistant. She's a writer and needs help with a book she's writing." Amanda walked to the living room and sat down on the couch. "I'm going to find out more tonight. I should probably get in the shower and start getting ready."

"Oh, you're not staying in?" Diane frowned. "That's too bad. I was looking forward to having some more fun with you." She took a sip of wine and licked her lips. "I can't stop thinking about last night. I love how you taste."

Amanda looked at the clock, then at Diane. The tops of her breasts peeked out of her white tank top, and her black denim shorts showed off her lean thighs. "I mean, I guess I don't have to leave just yet."

Diane set her wine down on the table, then sat on the couch and stroked Amanda's arm. "You think you could fit me into your busy schedule?"

Amanda smiled. "I think you could persuade me. But we need to make it quick."

"That sounds like a challenge." Diane leaned in and kissed her on the lips. "I love a challenge."

Amanda returned the kiss and slid a hand down Diane's thigh. "Times a-wastin'."

"Your place or mine?" Diane asked.

Amanda laughed. "My room." She led Diane down the hallway and pulled her into her bedroom. They flopped on the bed together and held each other for a moment.

"I want to eat you again so bad," Diane said. "I've been waiting to eat you all day."

Amanda smiled and slipped her pants off as Diane licked her fingers. She slid them inside Amanda's panties and stroked her labia. Amanda moaned and stroked her own breasts. Her nipples were hard, and she gently squeezed them.

Diane continued to stroke. "You're so wet already," she said.

"It's not my fault you turn me on so much," Amanda said. She squeezed her nipples again. "Fuck, that's good."

Diane found her nub and slid her finger across. Amanda tensed her body, then relaxed and spread her legs wide. "You found her."

Diane slowly removed her fingers and licked the juice from them.

"You're such a tease," Amanda said.

"Just switching gears," Diane said as she pulled Amanda's panties off. "This is what I really want." She grabbed Amanda's thighs and moved her face between her legs, exploring her pussy with her tongue.

"Yes," Amanda cried. "Right there."

Diane continued to lick, zeroing in on Amanda's clit and pressing down hard.

"Fuck, I'm going to come." Amanda arched her back, then rolled on to her side and softly stroked Diane's short, blond hair. They lay together for a moment in silence.

"I need to get ready for this dinner. I don't want to be late." Amanda sighed. "I could stay here with you all night."

"Dinner, huh? Where are you going?"

"I'm actually going up to her house," Amanda said. She rolled off the bed and slipped into her bathrobe.

"Oh? Does she this woman live close by?"

"No, she's somewhere up in Washington."

"How are you getting there? Do you need a ride?"

"No, her driver is picking me up."

Diane looked confused. "She has her own driver?"

"Yeah, wild, huh? Erica's great. I really hope this works out. It's such a great opportunity."

"You'll have to tell me all about it."

"Don't worry, I will."

"Cool, I guess I'll just watch a movie or something. Have fun at your fancy dinner, girl." Diane gave her ass a playful swat as they left the room together.

At exactly eight o'clock, the Mercedes pulled into the parking lot and Amanda walked out to meet it. She'd left Diane on the couch in pajamas, eating ice cream and watching one of those weird Japanese cartoons she loved so much.

Lawrence wore the same uniform he had previous night - black slacks and a pressed white shirt. Black bowtie. His shoes were black leather, polished to a shine and expensive. He was tall and broad-shouldered, but not imposing. There was a gentle quality about him that Amanda found comforting.

He got out and opened the door for her, as was his custom. "Good evening, Miss Amanda. Are you ready to experience Trent Manor?"

"I certainly am, Lawrence. Thank you."

Once inside, he got back in the driver's seat and pulled out of the parking lot. "Please call me Larry. Everyone does." He paused. "Everyone except Miss Erica, that is."

"Thanks, I will. And you can call me Amanda. No Miss necessary."

Lawrence laughed. "Thanks. I think I spend too much time around those fancy ladies. It becomes a habit. Yes, Miss Erica. Be right there, Miss Sylvie."

"I know what you mean," Amanda said. "When I'm waiting tables, I get in the zone. I feel like a robot. Like I'm just going through the motions."

"Oh, not me. Working for Miss Erica, it's something different every day. I never know where I'm going or who I'll be driving. One day I'm going up to Seattle to pick up one of her publisher friends at the airport. Next day, it's off to the coast to get fifty pounds of crab for the big party she's hosting. Tonight? Sylvie calls and tells me to go to Portland and fetch Miss Amanda." He paused and smiled, a genuine grin. "I'm sorry. Amanda. Anyway, it keeps it fresh."

"You do a lot of driving, then?"

"Oh, yes. Trent Manor has a lot of visitors. There's always someone coming or going. Sometimes they come up for the weekend, sometimes it's just an overnight stay. They're lovely women, all of them." He smiled at Amanda in the rear-view mirror. "I think you'd like them."

Lawrence merged onto I-5 North masterfully and increased speed. Amanda looked out the window as downtown flew past. "Open the refrigerator and get yourself a drink," he said. "We have a bit of a drive ahead of us. You might as well get comfortable."

There was a small fridge to her right. Amanda opened the door and took out a small bottle of white wine. She uncapped it, took a sip, and admired the label. "Not bad for a twist-off. Better than what I usually drink."

"Nothing but the best for Miss Erica," Lawrence said. "You'll see. There are glasses, you know."

"No, the bottle is fine for me. I'm not much for formality."

"I see why she likes you so much. You're different from the people who usually travel in these circles. Down to earth. I appreciate that."

Lawrence drove smoothly in the left lane. Amanda couldn't see how fast they were going, but they flew past the rest of the traffic. She leaned back and held on to her wine.

Is this really my life right now? I could get used to this.

Half an hour into their journey, Lawrence took an unmarked exit. Amanda hadn't been this far north in years and hadn't seen a town in miles. They drove through a dense canopy of trees, down a smooth, newly paved road.

After five minutes, Lawrence turned again and went straight up a hill until they reached the top. There, Amanda got her first look at Trent Manor.

This place should be a museum or something. She should charge admission.

Trent Manor sat near what looked like a small lake, dark and mysterious in the night. The house itself was enormous, with a circular driveway and a large white fountain in front. To the side of the main house were two smaller buildings and something looked like a tennis court. It was too dark to tell.

Lawrence stepped out of the car and walked around, but Amanda had already let herself out.

"You didn't wait for me to open the door for you," he said. "Usually they just sit there until I come around." Lawrence offered his arm, which she accepted. "At least let me walk you to the door." He rang the doorbell, then left her there and walked back to the car. "Enjoy your evening, Amanda," he said. "I'll pick you up after dinner."

An overhead light came on and the door opened. The woman who greeted her was in her late twenties or early thirties, her platinum blond hair tied up in a tight bun, immaculately dressed in a black and white maid outfit. She was a head shorter than Amanda, absolutely stunning in a cold, severe way, and didn't smile.

"Hi, I'm Amanda."

"Yes, Miss Trent is expecting you." She turned and stepped back into the house, and Amanda followed her inside. "I will serve dinner in half an hour. May I take your coat?"

"Thank you."

"I am Sylvie," the woman said. "I run this house, prepare the meals, and make sure all guests' needs are met. Miss Trent has told me to extend you every courtesy."

"That's very nice of you."

Sylvie looked away. "I do as she requests."

Wow. Okay, then.

Amanda handed her coat to Sylvie, who held it at arm's length before hanging it in a small room off to the side. "Follow me. Miss Trent will receive you in the upstairs parlor."

Amanda followed her, noting what a cute ass Sylvie had. Firm and toned, it fit her tight black skirt perfectly.

I can see why Erica keeps her on staff, even if she's a little rude. I'd keep beautiful women like her around me, too.

The house was even more impressive on the inside. Its walls were pure white, and collection of abstract paintings were prominently displayed. The front room was a reception area. There were a couple of large, soft-looking couches and a selection of magazines on a coffee table. They passed a formal dining room with a large table, and she followed Sylvie upstairs.

The second floor opened to another hallway. Sylvie led her past several closed doors and they turned right into yet another hallway, which turned into a mezzanine. It overlooked an open space the size of a small auditorium. There was a full bar and a dance floor. Along one wall ran a series of black leather couches. A television screen took up the opposite wall, with six-foot speakers on each side.

You could throw a hell of a party here. I see why Erica has so many guests. This place is party central.

Erica sat on a couch holding a glass of red wine. She looked radiant and relaxed. Her black top showed off her full breasts and just a hint of cleavage. Amanda walked toward her. The room was so large it took her a few moments to get there, so she had time to appreciate Erica's beauty.

Erica sat with her legs crossed, and Amanda noticed again how ample and firm her thighs were, tight in her black pants. A sexual spark- the passionate longing Erica ignited in her- rose again, and she tried to banish it from her mind.

So not the time for that. This is a job interview. Just play it cool, girl.

"Amanda, it's so lovely to see you again." Erica stood up to embrace her and immersed Amanda in her primal scent. The earthy musk drove her absolutely wild.

"Welcome to my home," Erica said. "I hope you'll enjoy yourself."

"It really is a palace. I love it."

"That's nice of you to say. It's the place I'm most comfortable in the world. It takes a lot of work to maintain a place this size, but I have an excellent staff. I expect Lawrence was good to you?"

"Oh, yes. He's such a gentleman."

"He certainly is. And you've met Sylvie, of course."

Sylvie stood at the edge of the room, awaiting orders.

"Would you like her to pour you a drink? Anything you'd like." Erica waved her arm at rows of liquor bottles. "If you can name it, she can make it."

Amanda paused, unsure.

"That's a yes. Sylvie, please fix Amanda a drink." She turned to Amanda. "How about a paloma? Do you like those?"

I've never even heard of them. But sure.

"If it's not too much trouble-" Amanda began.

Erica interrupted her. "It's no trouble at all. Sylvie, if you would."

Sylvie went behind the bar and had her drink prepared in a flash. She presented it to Amanda with a blank smile.

"Thank you very much. It looks wonderful."

"You're quite welcome, Miss Jones," Sylvie replied. She stood still and straight, staring ahead.

"You're dismissed, Sylvie," Erica said. "Please call us for dinner."

"Of course, ma'am." She bowed slightly and left.

Erica turned to Amanda and smiled. "Don't pay any attention to her. I know Sylvie can be moody sometimes, but she means well. She's been such a help to me, Amanda. I don't know what I would do without her. I'm sure you'll be good friends soon." She sat down on the couch and motioned for Amanda to join her. "I hate talking business over dinner, so would you like to get that out of the way now?"

"Of course."

"I've been ghostwriting for over a decade now," Erica began. "Some of my clients are quite famous, and a few of my titles have become bestsellers. You'd recognize some of their names, I'm sure." She crossed her legs, and Amanda instinctively followed them. Erica laughed.

Did she see me checking her out? I've got to get better at this.

"I could tell you stories," Erica continued, "of the things rich and powerful people do when they think no one's looking. It amazes me when people think they're above the law. But that's beside the point." She took a sip of wine. "It's completely anonymous work, which is wonderful. Fame doesn't suit me at all. And I've been able to build a good life for myself, as you can see."

"Yes, you have," Amanda agreed, and took a sip of her drink. It tasted like sweet grapefruit and was perfect.

"Not all this wealth comes from my writing business, of course. My parents were well-off to begin with, and I've made a few smart investments. Ghostwriting is almost a hobby for me. I like to keep my mind active. I have the freedom to choose the projects I work on, and this new one is very exciting. The woman who contacted me, Vivian Starr, owns the Obsidian Lounge. I assume you've heard of it?"

"I've heard stories," Amanda said, "but I've never been there. Don't you need an invitation to get in?"

"You do. They're extremely selective about who they let in. It's a very special place. Vivian wants to meet me tomorrow night in her office at the club. I'd like you to be there, if possible. Will you come?"

I'm going to see the inside of the Obsidian Lounge? This is amazing.

"Of course, I'd love to."

"Fantastic. Now, let's discuss salary. My standard rate for a research assistant is $1,200 a week. I pay all expenses when we travel, so hotels and meals will be provided when you're working. I expect that we're going to do a fair amount of travelling for this assignment." Erica leaned back and folder her hands. "How does that sound to you, Amanda?"

Amanda did some quick math in her head.

Sixty grand a year. This changes everything.

"It sounds amazing, Erica. Where do I sign?"

"Fabulous, I'm so glad." Erica smiled. "Now, transportation is going to be an issue. I've learned you don't drive, and I prefer to work from home. I don't mind sending Lawrence to get you for the time being. Eventually, we'll have to make other arrangements."

With the money I'll be making, I can afford a car. Maybe even something that isn't a beater.

"Let's not worry about it right now," Erica continued. "We'll have plenty of time to figure all that out. The important thing is that you can start immediately. Vivian is eager to begin work."

Sylvie announced her return with a loud knock on the door. "Dinner is served, Miss Erica."

"Thank you, Sylvie. We'll be right down." Erica stood up and Amanda followed her lead. "Bring your drink. I'll give you a tour of the second floor."

They walked back through the mezzanine and down the hallway.

"The second floor is mainly bedrooms and offices." Erica pointed to the end of the hallway. "My office is down there. It has the most wonderful view of the garden and the lake." She opened a door on the right. "And this is the office you'll be using. It doesn't have as nice of a view, but it's still quite pleasant. Wouldn't you say?"

Amanda poked her head inside. The room almost as big as her apartment. A large, modern desk with a computer looked out to the grounds. Bookshelves lined the walls. There was a stocked pantry with a coffeemaker, microwave and a small refrigerator. A new, top-of-the-line exercise bike sat in the far corner.

"This is all for me?" she asked, shocked.

"Of course. You need someplace to work, and you're going to be very busy. Vivian wants to release this book as soon as possible."

They continued down the hall, and Erica pointed up a flight of carpeted stairs. "My room is on the third floor. I have a sauna and a hot tub, a few other toys. It's a great place to entertain my guests. Very private." She smiled at Amanda. "It's not all work around here, you know."

Erica led her downstairs, through a large industrial kitchen, and into the dining room. Sylvie had prepared a wonderful dinner for them. Shrimp cocktail and crab bisque, for starters, with freshly baked rolls. The main course was a small steak, new potatoes, and vegetables. It was one of the best meals she'd had in her life.

Beats a greasy burger and soggy fries from Sam's Clubhouse, that's for sure.

Sylvie was an attentive server, and Amanda drank two glasses of delicious, dark red wine she poured as Erica enthralled her with stories about her life and career.

"Excuse us, Amanda," Erica said once dinner was over, "please wait in the parlor. I have a matter to attend to with Sylvie. Lawrence should be here soon to drive you home. If he doesn't, find us and I'll have Sylvie call him."

"Of course. Thanks again for everything."

"I look forward to working with you," Erica said. "Good night."

She turned, and Sylvie followed her out. Amanda watched them until they disappeared up the stairs.

The meal had been excellent, and she had a bit of a buzz going. Full and satisfied, slightly tipsy. The light in the reception room was soft and warm, and she sat on a couch and started thumbing through the current issue of Entertainment Weekly.

I should have asked where the bathroom is. It's a long drive back to the city.

She got up and explored Trent Manor, opening a few doors. No bathroom, but she was amazed at how clean everything was. She admired the paintings on the walls and a large aquarium she discovered in one of the rooms.

Maybe upstairs?

She passed a few closed doors, then her new office. There was an open restroom across the hall.

Wow, that's convenient. This job is getting better and better.

The restroom exceeded her expectations. Pristine and warm, with a large mirror and soft towels for her hands. When she finished, she sat for a moment taking in the luxury of it all. As she closed the door behind her, she heard voices from the direction of the dance room. Curious, she walked to the end of the hall and toward the mezzanine. From there, she had an overview of the entire room. What she saw stopped her in her tracks.

Erica and Sylvie stood facing each other in the middle of the room. Sylvie had taken her top off, her small, firm breasts clearly visible. She still wore her tight black maid's skirt, and Amanda noticed again what a cute, firm ass she had. She had let her long, blond hair out of its bun, and it cascaded past her shoulders.

Erica turned Sylvie around and stood behind her. She took Sylvie's bare breasts in her hands, making slow circles with her palms. Without warning, she spun Sylvie around and pushed her toward the floor.

Amanda took a few steps back and crouched in the darkness of the mezzanine. She didn't know if they could see her, and her heart pounded with fear and excitement.

Sylvie, now on her knees, took Erica's legs in her hands, rubbing them up and down with slow strokes, nuzzling Erica's thighs with her cheeks.

"Would you like a taste, my pet?" Erica asked. "Of course you would. It's what you live for. You're my good girl."

"Yes, mistress. Please. I've waited for this all night." Sylvie pawed at the front of Erica's pants, seeking entrance.

Erica slipped her pants and panties off, revealing strong, pale thighs and a dark mound of pubic hair. It was the most gorgeous bush Amanda had ever seen, and Sylvie went at it, licking her eagerly.

Erica sat on one of the black leather couches and allowed herself to be pleasured. Sylvie obviously had a practiced technique. Erica threw her head back and moaned in delight. She licked her fingers and played with her nipples, flicking and squeezing them as she arched her back and pressed herself hard against Sylvie's mouth.

Amanda's hand went to her pants, and she touched herself out of pure instinct.

Wow, that wine went to my head. And this is so hot.

She rubbed herself as she watched the action below. Slipping a hand in her panties, she guided it to her pussy, already wet, then stopped.

I should just go back downstairs. I'm not supposed to be seeing this.

Erica's moans strengthened as Sylvie increased speed, and Amanda couldn't look away. She had wondered about Erica from the moment she'd seen her- what sort of sexual creature she was- and wasn't disappointed. Erica owned her sexuality completely.

"Stop," Erica said. Sylvie slowed down and lowered her head. "Did you hear something?"

Sylvie turned toward the mezzanine and peered into the darkness.

Busted. Shit, how am I going to explain this?

Amanda pulled her hand back and stood still. She held her breath and waited in silence.

"I didn't hear anything," Sylvie said, after what seemed like an eternity.

"Very well," Erica said, "you may continue."

Amanda exhaled slowly.

Sylvie redoubled her efforts, grabbing Erica's ass with both hands and going deeper with her tongue.

How does she lick so fast? My mouth's getting tired just watching her.

Amanda reached down to touch herself again, and her pussy responded immediately. She found her clit and rubbed in a soft circle. Keeping time with the scene below her, she pleasured herself vigorously until her fingers were wet with her juices.

That should really be me down there. I could show them a thing or two.

To see a woman as exquisite as Erica get eaten out was like a dream come true for her. Sylvie's ass rose up as she licked Erica's pussy, and Amanda watched with admiration. Her nipples were hard now. She took one in her fingers and gave it a twist. Pleasure soared as she rubbed her clit with her other hand.

Below, Erica writhed on the couch in ecstasy. Rocking back and forth, she built to a tremendous orgasm. "Yes, Sylvie. Make me come."

Amanda watched the expression on Erica's face, absolute bliss. Sylvie earned her keep, sucking Erica's pussy in a frenzy of motion.

Oh fuck. I'm going to come, too.

Her breath sped up, the heat swelled inside her, and the orgasm built to a peak until she gave in to it. With a final throb, she came in silent waves.

Afterward, Erica sat on the couch and lazily rubbed Sylvie's saliva on her thighs. After a few moments, she spoke. "Put your shirt back on, Sylvie," she said. "Call Lawrence and have him drive Amanda home. She must be bored to tears downstairs."

"Why can't she wait a little longer?" Sylvie murmured. "She's not going anywhere."

"Play nice, Sylvie. You're going to have to get along with her. I won't let you run her off like you did the last one. I need her."

"You need me, too," Sylvie said.

Erica stroked her hair and smiled. "You know I do. You're my best girl." Erica stood up. "Still, playtime is over now. Please do as I ask."

Sylvie sighed. "Yes, mistress." She stood up and picked her bra and white shirt off the floor. She put the bra on, buttoned her shirt back up, and walked toward the mezzanine, toward Amanda.

40

Shit! I'd better get back downstairs quick.

Amanda turned and crept quietly down the hall, down the stairs, and into the waiting room. She was picking up the magazine again when Lawrence arrived.

"Ready to go home, Amanda?" Larry was still in his chauffeur uniform, ready for duty. "I was told you were ready."

"Yes, I just need to grab my coat."

"Allow me." He retrieved her jacket from the coatroom and handed it to her. "There you are." He reached into his pocket and handed her an envelope. "Miss Erica told me to give this to you. Your instructions for tomorrow night are inside."

"Thank you, Larry." The envelope was thick, high-quality paper, and she stuck it in her coat pocket.

"The car is waiting. Shall we?"

The apartment was dark and quiet when Amanda got home.

Diane must be asleep. I can't wait to tell her what happened tonight. And the Obsidian Lounge. She's going to freak.

She looked at the clock.

Midnight already. Where did the night go?

She thought back on the sexual spectacle she'd witnessed that evening and smiled to herself.

That seemed like a normal occurrence at Trent Manor. This job is going to be interesting.

Lawrence steered the Mercedes confidently through the parking structure and made a slow, winding journey down three levels. He parked by the entrance, where an attractive young woman stood surrounded by a small group of well-dressed ladies. She wore a headset and held some sort of scanner. One by one she beeped their phones. They walked through the door laughing and smiling.

Amanda had walked past the Obsidian Lounge a hundred times, but never knew about its secret underground entrance. She felt like she was part of an exclusive club now.

I can't believe I'm going inside. Now I'll see if all those stories are true.

Lawrence got out of the car and opened the back door for Amanda and Erica. Erica wore a tight, black dress that showed off her lovely thighs and hips, a black hat, and her usual silver jewelry. Amanda hadn't been sure how to dress and had debated for a long time earlier in the evening, finally deciding on a pair of black pants and white blouse she'd bought for a job interview last year.

"This is where we take our leave of you," Erica told Lawrence. "Ladies only past this point."

"Of course, I understand," Lawrence said. "Have a good meeting with Ms. Starr. I'll keep my phone on me and wait for your call."

"I don't know how long we'll be tonight. It could be a couple of hours, or it might be longer. Since it's Amanda's first time here, we could end up staying a while." She gave Amanda a sly smile.

"Call when you're ready and I'll come right back," Lawrence said. He bowed slightly and returned to the car.

"Well, my dear, are you ready to experience the Obsidian Lounge?" Erica offered her arm to Amanda. It was strong and warm, and she accepted it with pleasure.

"Lead the way, Miss Erica."

The door girl wore a walkie-talkie on the hip of her short, red dress. She was confident and self-assured, her dark hair tucked under a white wool beret.

"Good evening, ladies," she greeted them. "Do you have an invitation tonight? Are you on our list?"

"We have an appointment with Miss Starr," Erica told her. "She's expecting us."

The door girl smiled. "Oh, you must be Ms. Trent. Yes, Vivian asked me to keep an eye out for you. It's so nice of you to come down." She turned to Amanda. "And who is your lovely companion?"

"This is my assistant, Amanda."

"It's a pleasure to meet you both. The offices are on the bottom level of the club, and the easiest way to get there is straight through the bar. I'll page someone to accompany you down. One moment, please." She pressed a button on her walkie and spoke into the headset. "Downstairs escort to the lower entrance, please. Downstairs escort."

She shut the walkie off and turned back to them. "Someone will be right up. The club has many levels, many rooms. You could get lost without a guide."

"Wouldn't that be a pity?" Erica murmured, smiling mischievously.

She's like an excited child tonight. Adorable.

The front door opened, and a young woman stepped out. She was in her early twenties, with short spiky blonde hair, and wore a white top and a black mini-skirt. Her crimson-red boots reached all the way up her legs.

I like your style, girl. A little punk, but subtle. Good job.

"Sapphire, this is Ms. Trent and her assistant, Amanda," the door girl said. "Please walk them to the South elevator. Ms. Starr is expecting them."

"It will be a pleasure," Sapphire said. "Please come with me, and welcome to the Obsidian Lounge."

She held the door open, and Amanda and Erica followed her inside.

Loud dance music played inside. Sapphire led them through a sea of bodies. There was a bar on each side of the large room, a long line at each. Gorgeous bartenders worked hard to keep the drinks flowing. There were two stages in the club, and the dancers slid down poles or chatted among themselves. A metal cage hung from the ceiling. Inside, a lady in a catsuit simulated masturbation while a crowd of women fed bills through the bars.

This place is wild. It just gets better and better.

"What do you think? Is it what you expected?" Erica asked, and squeezed Amanda's arm. Amanda grabbed hold of her. Erica comforting, a familiar presence in the new environment.

"I could get lost in here," she said. "It's amazing."

"Isn't it?" Erica pulled her in closer and spoke in her ear as they followed Sapphire through the bar. "Oh, the fun I've had here. The stories I could tell you about my younger days." She leaned in close, her breath warm on Amanda's ear. "Maybe someday I will."

They exited the bar and walked down a hallway as the lights and music faded into the background. They stopped in front of an elevator, and Sapphire pressed a button. When the door opened, Sapphire pressed another series of buttons on the wall and stepped back outside.

"This takes you to the offices," she told them. "Check in with Clara when you get downstairs." She hitched up her boots, sliding her hands up her legs and showing a flash of her inner thighs. "Maybe I'll see you two later. I'll be on the south stage in an hour."

"How delightful," Erica said. "We'll keep an eye out for you."

The elevator took them down two levels, and the door opened to a large waiting room. It was silent and modern, a sharp contrast from the carnival going on upstairs. Clara sat behind a desk. She was in her mid-twenties and gorgeous, with long blond hair and thick, black-framed glasses. She looked up from her computer and greeted them.

"You must be Miss Trent," she said.

"Yes, but please call me Erica. This is my research assistant, Amanda."

"Welcome to the business offices. We don't have nearly as much fun as they do upstairs, but someone has to do the paperwork. I'll tell Vivian you've arrived." She picked up the phone, pressed a button, and spoke into it. "Miss Trent is here."

Clara pointed to a door. "Her office is down the hall at the end. Last door on the right. It was nice to meet you both."

"You, too," Amanda said, opening the door for Erica.

Vivian's office door was wide open, but Erica knocked anyway.

"Come in, ladies," Vivian called. She slid a pile of papers away from her desk and stood up to meet them. "Thanks again for meeting me outside business hours. I appreciate it."

Vivian was in her late forties. Her straight, copper hair was cut short, and she dressed sensibly in business casual, a white button-down top and black pants.

She must have been a fox when she was younger. And she still looks damn good.

"I couldn't pass up an opportunity to come back here," Erica said.

"Oh?" Vivian smiled. "You've been to the Obsidian before? I didn't know that."

"Indeed, maybe ten years ago. It's a delightful place. I enjoyed myself very much."

"I'm glad to hear that, Erica. I hope you find the opportunity to enjoy yourself again. We offer a variety of options here, something for everyone." Vivian looked over at Amanda. "Is this lovely young woman your research assistant?"

"Yes, this is Amanda Jones." Erica smiled at Amanda. "She just started with me, but I already know she's going to be tremendously helpful."

"Thank you for inviting me," Amanda said.

"Of course," Vivian said. "I want you to be aware of everything from the beginning, so it's good you're both here."

"So, what have you got?" Erica asked. "What's this book about?"

"Right to business," Vivian said. "That's an admirable trait, Erica." She closed her laptop and set the stack of papers on her desk on a nearby table. "I've been sitting here staring at that computer all day, and I'm done. Can I offer you a drink? You know, there's a bar upstairs." She laughed. "And I just happen to own it."

"Lovely. Amanda, would you care for a drink?" Erica asked.

"Are you going to have one?"

Vivian laughed. "You two are impossible," she exclaimed. She pressed a button on her phone and spoke into it. "Clara, bring a bottle of white wine and three glasses, please. Thank you." She leaned back in her chair and smiled. "Clara is a wonderful young woman. I'm lucky to have her. Sharp as a tack, that one."

"All the women we've met tonight have been delightful," Erica said. "Beyond helpful, and pleasant."

"I take pride in my lounge and want it to be a great place to work," Vivian said. "That's why I contacted you, Erica. It's finally time for me to tell the true story of the Obsidian. There have been so many rumors, speculation, and outright lies over the years, and I want to set the record straight. You come highly recommended from a mutual friend, and I know you'll be able to help me craft a great narrative." She turned to Amanda. "Have you ever been here, dear?" she asked.

"I've known about the Obsidian for years, but have never been inside until tonight," Amanda admitted. "It's always been a dream of mine to be invited."

"Well, the Obsidian is a place where fantasies come true and no questions are asked. Do you understand?"

"Yes."

"That's good. When people are open-minded about these things, it makes everything so much easier."

There was a knock on the door, and Clara walked in carrying a tray with a bottle of wine and three glasses. She set the tray down on a table and uncorked the bottle.

"Glasses all around?" she asked.

"Yes, please," Vivian said.

Clara handed a glass first to Vivian, then to Erica and Amanda.

"You're going to see these two around here a lot in the next couple of months," Vivian told Clara. "Please extend them every courtesy. I want them granted full access to every level of the building."

"Of course," Clara said. She bowed slightly and smiled at them. "If you need anything, just ask." She left, shutting the door behind her.

Vivian raised her glass. "A toast. To new partnerships."

Erica and Amanda raised their glasses and drank. The wine was ice cold and crisp. Amanda knew nothing about wine but could tell it was high quality.

Probably ridiculously expensive, too.

It tickled her nose, and she suppressed a giggle.

"I want to tell the true story of the club for the first time," Vivian continued. "Uncensored and real. How I built it into what it is now, the fights I had with the city, all of it. I know a few people won't be happy with it, but I already have a publisher eager to release it. I just need someone to help me put it together, and that's where you two come in."

"Where would you like to start?" Erica asked. "I know several ways to compose these types of narratives."

"Many of my girls are interested in being interviewed. Some have retired and moved on to new careers, while others still work here. I've set up a half-dozen interviews over the next few weeks to get you started." Vivian took a sip of wine. "Of course, I also want to tell my story. I want to get started on this as soon as possible. Honestly, I would be most comfortable at my home on the coast. It seems to be the only place I can relax anymore. If you're available, I'd like to invite you there this weekend."

"That will be no problem," Erica assured her. She turned to Amanda. "You don't have plans, do you?"

A trip to the coast? Count me in.

"No, no plans."

"This is my specialty," Erica told Vivian, "gathering source material and creating a quality manuscript. I can't wait to get started."

"Fabulous," Vivian said. "Shall I send my driver tomorrow?"

Erica laughed. "Oh, Vivian. You must know I have my own driver. Lawrence is indispensable and goes with me everywhere."

"Of course, how silly of me. Well, the house has five guest rooms, so you'll be quite comfortable."

"I'll arrange Lawrence's lodging. I'll have my girl Sylvie reserve a nice room for him in town."

"Very well, it's settled. I look forward to getting to know you both better over the weekend." Vivian set her empty wine glass on her desk. "I have a few things to finish up here, so I'll say goodbye for now." She buzzed her desk again. "Clara, will you see them out, please?"

Back in the outer offices, Clara rose from her desk and Amanda couldn't help but admire her figure.

That secretary is something else. I hope I get to see her again soon.

"I meant what I said in there," Clara told them. "I know the club intimately and can be very helpful with research. If you need anything at all, please ask."

"We will, dear," Erica said. "Thank you."

Amanda and Erica took the elevator up and made their way back to the club. The loud music and flashing lights of the dance floor beckoned again.

Maybe that cage act is still going on. I could get into that.

"Amanda, would you care to join me for a drink?" Erica asked. "Being here again has brought up some wonderful memories, and I'd like to stay a little longer."

"I've been wanting to come here for years," Amanda said. "A drink sounds wonderful."

"Splendid, I'll lead the way."

Erica guided her through the crowd. Between the women dancing on stage, the long line at the bar, and the sweet smell of perfume and sweat, the Obsidian Lounge was a sensory overload. Erica made eye contact with a bartender, who raced over to take their order. In a few minutes, they had vodka-7s in their hands.

"How did you do that?" Amanda asked in astonishment. "I thought we were going wait for hours."

"I never think about it," Erica said. "I expect to be served, and people respond to me. It works quite well." She smiled. "You should try it yourself sometime." She took Amanda's hand again, giving it a gentle squeeze. "Come with me. I know where I want to go."

On the main stage, a burlesque revue was in full swing. A row of topless dancers kicked their legs in unison, their outfits exotic and sensual. There were also several smaller stages off to the side, and Erica led Amanda to one of them. They sat down and set their drinks in front of them.

The dancer on stage spun down from the top of the pole, sliding down in one fluid movement until she reached the floor, then made her way over to them.

"Good evening, ladies. Are you enjoying yourselves tonight?"

"Very much," Erica said. She reached into her purse, pulled out a twenty, and set it on the stage. "How are you, dear?"

"Better now that you two are here." She pawed the bill toward the center of the stage and pulled herself up on the rack, then leaned in close and slowly rubbed herself on Erica.

"Oh, my goodness," Erica exclaimed. "Aren't you a frisky one? I love it."

The dancer smiled seductively and made her way back to the pole. She spun around over and over until the song was over.

"Thank you, ladies," she said as she walked off.

Next up was Sapphire. Amanda watched as she approached the stage with confidence. She had changed her outfit but kept the red boots.

Sexy as hell. Man, those boots are hot.

Erica touched Amanda's arm. "Look who it is. Aren't we in luck?" She took two more twenties out and set them on the stage.

Sapphire saw them and waved. She started her set with a quick spin around the pole and walked over. "I was hoping I'd see you two again. How was your meeting with Vivian?"

"Exceptional," Erica said. "We're going to stay for a while. I forgot how fantastic this place is."

Sapphire turned her attention to Amanda. "And you? How do you like our little club so far?"

"I love it. It's like a dream."

"Isn't it? I love it, too. You're just in time for my set." She turned around, flashing her ass at them, and crawled up the pole. She slid down slowly and gracefully and danced her way toward them.

"Do you see that?" Erica asked. "That's talent. It's incredible what these dancers can do on stage." She took a sip of her drink. "Makes you wonder what else she can do."

Amanda looked at Erica, who smiled slyly.

"So, what do you think?" Erica asked. "Do you like her?"

"Oh, yes. She's a wonderful dancer."

"Wonderful dancer," Erica repeated. "Yes, she is that." She motioned to Sapphire, who danced her way across the stage and lay down in front of them. The next song started, an old hair metal ballad. "Sapphire, I want to ask. Are you available for private dances?"

Sapphire's eyes lit up. "I certainly am. I'm actually known for them."

"Excellent," Erica said. She put her arm around Amanda. "She's all yours. Show her the time of her life, please."

Sapphire looked at Amanda with clear blue eyes and smiled. "Ooh, this one. It will be a pleasure."

"Wonderful."

Two ladies sat down on the other side of the stage, and Sapphire walked over to show them some attention.

"What are you doing?" Amanda whispered.

"You told me you liked her."

"Well, of course. She's fabulous."

"Well, nothing. You're going to have a good time tonight, I'll to see to that. You want your first night at the Obsidian to be special, right? One you'll never forget?"

Amanda nodded.

"Don't worry about me. I can easily entertain myself." Erica looked around the bar at the various stages. The burlesque show was still going on and had only gotten louder and more crowded. It was standing room only around the stage, women throwing bills at the dancers' feet. "In fact, I believe I will. You have a little fun. She's a cutie."

The song ended, and Sapphire came back over to them. Erica reached in her purse and produced two hundreds. "Will this be sufficient?" she asked.

Sapphire slid the bills into one of her boots. "More than sufficient," she said. "Come along, Amanda. I'll give you a private tour of the back room. Bring your drink."

The next dancer came on stage, a tall brunette wearing a cowboy hat. She smiled as she danced over to Erica.

"Maybe I'll just stay here for the next set," Erica said, sliding another twenty on the stage. "You two enjoy yourselves."

Sapphire picked up her bills from the stage and put them in her boot. She led Amanda through the bar, grabbing two bottles of water from a cooler on the way.

"These are complementary for the dancers," she explained. "Have to stay hydrated, you know. You'll be glad afterward. Trust me." She put her arm around Amanda and they walked out of the main bar.

They went down a hallway, turned a corner, and ended up in a large room with doors on each of its four walls. One had a red light above it, the other three lights were green. Sapphire went to one with a green light and entered a code on a keypad. The door opened, and Amanda followed her inside.

Soft blue light covered every surface of the room. Inside was a plush two-seat couch and a small table for drinks.

"I'm glad this one was open," Sapphire said. "I love the Water Room."

"This is so cool," Amanda said. "It's like being at the bottom of the ocean."

"The private rooms all have a different theme. On this floor, each room corresponds to one of the four elements. The Fire Room is intense. I would have brought you there, but it's occupied. The upper floors also have their own themes."

Sapphire pointed out the aquarium built into the wall. Schools of fish swam around sunken castles. "Amazing, right?"

"It really is."

"Get comfortable, Amanda. You're in good hands." Sapphire stretched and touched her toes. "I've got to stretch. Pole work is hard on the legs."

"It's impressive," Amanda said. "You make it look easy."

"Thanks." Sapphire listened to the music for a moment. "We'll wait until the next song starts. I'm supposed to charge by the song." She smiled. "But with what Erica paid me, we could be here a while. Let's enjoy ourselves." Sapphire sat down on the couch next to her. "You know, you're cute."

"So are you."

"This is going to be fun." Sapphire turned and faced Amanda. "So, what are you into? Do you like to watch? Maybe something more? That's the great thing about this place, there are no limits." The song started, and Sapphire stood up. "Relax, I'll take care of you."

Amanda let herself sink into the sofa as Sapphire danced in beat with the song. Sapphire pulled her shirt over her head, offering a glimpse of her small, perky tits, then quickly covered herself again.

"Like what you see?"

"Lovely," Amanda said.

"Thank you. I used to think they were too small, but now I appreciate them. I know some of the other girls have implants, but I don't know if I could do that."

"You don't need to. They're fantastic just how they are."

Sapphire gave another peek and slowly rubbed her hands down her shirt. Amanda noted her hard nipples poking out and wondered what they'd feel like in her mouth.

I'm going to get myself in trouble if I don't watch it.

"I've never had a private dance before," Amanda admitted.

"Really?" Sapphire smiled with a gleam in her eye. "Why didn't you say so?" Sapphire danced closer. "I'll make this one extra special."

A sensual heat came from Sapphire, and Amanda felt a familiar stir in her center. Sapphire slid toward the floor, her chest getting within inches, and continued to dance.

Amanda sighed in frustration, and Sapphire laughed.

"That's why it's called a striptease. The anticipation can be so powerful."

"I feel it."

"I've noticed." She swept over again, brushing herself against Amanda's nipples, which were also getting hard. "It's normal. In fact, it's expected." She pulled back and smiled. "And, in this case, it's encouraged. I love arousing women. I get off on it too, you know."

"You do?" Amanda tensed, waiting for the next pass.

"Of course. Why else do you think I do this? Yes, the money's great. But turning someone on just using my body and my mind? That's some empowering stuff."

Sapphire slid off again and stood up as the song faded out. "What do you think? Having fun?"

"Oh, yes."

"I'm so glad. I can always tell when someone's not into it. It's so discouraging. It makes me work twice as hard."

"You don't make it seem like work at all."

Sapphire looked into her eyes. "Sometimes it isn't."

The next song came on. Sapphire started out slowly, removing her shirt. This time it stayed off, and she threw it next to the couch. She cupped her breasts in her hands and rolled her palms over her nipples. Amanda's hand instinctively reached down to touch herself, but she resisted and brought it back up.

Sapphire pinched her nipples as she headed straight for Amanda. She straddled her and rubbed herself all over. One of Sapphire's nipples brushed Amanda's cheek and she couldn't help herself. She stuck her tongue out and flicked it, a slight graze.

Oops! I can't believe I did that.

"Oh, naughty," Sapphire said. She thrust her hips harder and rocked herself back and forth on Amanda's lap. "I love it."

Amanda took another lick, longer and slower this time. She swirled her tongue around Sapphire's nipple and pulled back.

"Taste good?" Sapphire asked.

Amanda nodded yes.

"You can play with me. It's okay."

Amanda cupped Sapphire's breasts with her hands.

"There you go. You can do more, you know." Sapphire took Amanda's hand and licked her palm, then placed it on her breast. "Like that."

Amanda licked her fingers and plucked one of her own nipples, which were still hard and eager.

"Now you're getting it."

Sapphire slid her hands under Amanda's ass and rubbed her cheeks. With each pass, she got closer and closer to Amanda's pussy.

This is fucking wild, and I love it.

The song faded out, and Sapphire slowly slid off.

"You're amazing," Amanda said.

"You're pretty fun yourself." Sapphire uncapped a bottle of water and took a sip. "I told you I'd show you a good time."

"You weren't lying."

The next song came on, an old Rolling Stones tune from the seventies.

"I love this one," Sapphire said.

"Yes, I love the Stones. They're one of my favorites."

Sapphire started on the ground this time. She lifted herself up and pressed hard against Amanda's lap. Her tits were at eye-level, and Amanda took one in her mouth. She twirled Sapphire's nipple with her tongue and slid a hand down to touch her ass. She started to rub, but Sapphire moved her hand to Amanda's thigh and held it there.

"Tonight is about you," she said.

Amanda moved her hand to her lap and felt the heat rising. She was wet now, ready for more.

Sapphire leaned in and whispered. "It's okay, baby. Go for it. I want you to."

Amanda quickly unbuttoned her pants and slid two fingers down her panties. She easily found her clit and her pleasure grew.

It feels so natural. Like this was supposed to happen.

"That's good. Just like that," Sapphire said.

Amanda continued to stroke herself. Her breathing became faster as the speed increased. She took one of Sapphire's nipples in her mouth and squeezed it between her lips. Sapphire moaned, continuing to grind against her.

"You're so hot right now, you know that? Damn." Sapphire reached under Amanda's shirt, found a nipple, and squeezed hard.

Shock waves raced through her body. "Yes, do that," Amanda said. "Please."

Sapphire laughed. "Gladly."

Amanda grabbed her other nipple and played with it. Now she had three hands working her. She arched her back, rubbing her clit in quick circles. Her climax worked toward its peak, and she moaned in delight.

"Are you going to come now, baby? Come for me." Sapphire kissed her, rolling her tongue around and sending Amanda into overdrive.

"Do it. I want you to. Come for me."

Amanda came, a blazing orgasm that surged through her body. She collapsed onto the sofa as the song faded out.

Sapphire offered her a sip of water, which she gladly accepted. "See, I knew you'd want this."

Amanda laughed. "You were so right."

Erica had moved to the front of the club and was deep in conversation with the bartender. The room had cleared while they'd been in the back and the night seemed to be winding down.

"There you are," Erica said as they approached. "I trust you had a good time?"

Amanda smiled bashfully, still energized and tingling from her orgasm. She wiped the sweat off the back of her neck.

"Where did you find this girl?" Sapphire asked. "She's fantastic!"

"Isn't she? I'm becoming quite fond of her myself. She's such a great addition to my team." Erica finished her drink. "Lawrence is on his way. He'll text once he's outside." She gave Amanda a sly smile. "Look at you. You look a little flushed. I guess you really did enjoy yourself."

"She did," Sapphire said. "I made sure of it."

Erica winked at her. "I'm glad she got the full Obsidian experience. We're going to be coming here a lot over the next few months. It's important that she knows everything that's available to her."

"That's wonderful," Sapphire said. "Come back and visit anytime. You too, Erica." She gave Amanda a hug. "I should get changed, my shift almost over. I hope I see you again soon."

So do I. This place is so much better than I could have even imagined. And I can imagine a lot.

Erica's phone buzzed. "There he is. Are you ready, Amanda? Do you have everything?" She walked toward the exit and Amanda followed.

"Lawrence will drop you off at your apartment tonight," Erica told her once they were back in the car. "Take tomorrow morning off. Sleep in and take care of any personal business you have. We'll leave in the afternoon and won't be back until

Sunday, so pack accordingly. Vivian has booked us a trip to a private spa, which I'm so looking forward to. If it's the place I think it is, we're in for a special treat."

She clapped her hands together and squealed with delight. "Oh, I love the coast. This is going to be so much fun!"

Amanda woke the next morning still excited and turned-on from last night at the Obsidian. Since she was free of Sam's Clubhouse, she had the morning free to pack and prepare for her trip to the coast. She rolled out of bed and brushed her teeth, then started a pot of coffee.

How is this even my life right now? I can't believe it.

She heard the shower running and realized she hadn't seen Diane since the night they had gotten together.

Has it only been three days? It feels like a lifetime ago. So much has happened.

As she waited for the coffee to finish brewing, she heard the shower stop.

I know. I'll make breakfast before she goes to work.

There was a bag of hash browns in the freezer and a half-carton of eggs in the fridge. The package of English muffins on the counter were still soft, so they were probably fine. She got to work.

"What are you doing?" Diane asked as she walked into the living room dressed for another day in the coffee shop. Tight black jeans, Doc Martens, a dark blue cardigan, and a Blondie t-shirt.

"I thought I'd make breakfast for us. Do you want some?"

Diane poured a cup of coffee and stood in the kitchen. "That's nice of you. Yeah, I should probably eat. I'm so tired of everything at work. You can only eat so many bagels, you know." She reached in the fridge for the half-and-half. "How are you doing? You okay?"

Amanda smiled, remembering how hard she had come with Sapphire last night. "Better than okay. This new job is turning into way more than I expected."

"Yeah? All kinds of fancy writerly things?"

"No writing yet. Erica took me to the Obsidian Lounge last night."

"Really, the Obsidian? Wow, that takes me back."

"You've been?"

Diane nodded. "Oh yeah. I had some wild nights there with Celeste. You remember her, right?"

"Of course. You two were the perfect couple."

"We were, weren't we? I can't believe she got away." She thought for a moment. "I should call and see how she's doing. We really haven't talked in a while. Maybe she can get me on the list or something. I'll bet she still knows people there."

"You should definitely go if you can. I had a great time. It's so wild."

"Did you get one of the private dances?"

Amanda nodded, thinking back on how Sapphire had straddled her and let her suck on her tits.

I can't believe what I got away with. I probably broke a half dozen rules last night.

"Aren't they amazing?"

"Out of this world," Amanda agreed.

"So, are you staying in tonight, or going out?" Diane asked. She leaned against the counter expectantly and took a sip of coffee.

"I actually have to leave again this afternoon."

"For work? You work strange hours."

"Erica's excited to get started on the project."

"This is for the woman who owns the Obsidian?"

"Vivian Starr, yeah. She's really cool."

"I'll bet. I've only ever heard about her." Diane scooped another spoonful of sugar into her coffee and stirred. "I hate to change the subject, but are you getting paid soon? The first is coming up and I don't have enough to float us both."

Oh, shit. I haven't even thought to ask about money. It's kind of hard when Erica is spending hundreds on private dances for me.

"I'll ask her today. She said I'll get paid every week."

"Cool."

"So, how do you want your eggs?"

"Scrambled with cheese?"

"You got it."

Amanda cracked the eggs into a bowl and began whisking them with half and half.

Lawrence and Erica picked her up at noon. Lawrence took her roller bag and backpack and set them in the roomy cargo area next to Erica's luggage.

"Good afternoon, Amanda," he said. "I hope you slept well."

"I did. Thanks, Larry. You look sharp as ever."

"Smoke and mirrors, my dear. It's all an act, but don't you dare tell Miss Erica." He laughed and held the back door open.

Erica sat in the back, put together as usual, her dark blue dress accenting her breasts and legs in all the right ways. She wore sunglasses and sipped from a blue glass.

"Tell me what?" she asked.

"Wouldn't you like to know?" Lawrence countered. He shut the door and walked around to the driver's side.

"He's been in such a mood lately," Erica said. "So much saucier than usual."

"I heard that," Lawrence said, and put the car in drive.

Erica leaned back in her seat and shifted her legs toward Amanda. "When was the last time you visited the coast? Has it been a while?"

Amanda thought back. "Yeah. I went a few times with my girlfriends back in college, but since I graduated I've just been working. It's hard to get away."

"Well, I'm going to change all that. Starting now. I've been looking forward to this very much." She took a sip of her drink. "Sylvie was thoughtful enough to send us off with fresh-squeezed lemonade for our trip. It has ginger and ginseng in it, very healthy. You should try some."

"Thank you, I will."

Erica poured a small amount into a cup and handed it to her. She took a hesitant sip, but it was good. Strong and tart, with just a hint of sweetness.

Fuck it, this is as good a time as any.

"Erica?"

"Yes, Amanda? What is it?"

"I hate to bring it up now, but do you know when I'll be getting my first paycheck?"

"Oh, my goodness." Erica giggled. "I'd completely forgotten. Sylvie usually handles these things for me. Of course. I'll call tonight and have her set it up for you. I'm so sorry, Amanda."

"It's no problem. I just wanted to be sure."

"Thank you for reminding me." Erica turned to her, her cleavage exposed, and Amanda had to force herself not to stare. "Are you all right? Do you need something to tide you over? It's no problem for me."

"Oh, no," Amanda reassured her. "It's just that rent is coming up, and Diane asked when I'd have my share."

"Diane is your roommate?"

"Yes, my roommate and a good friend from college."

"I see. Well, it's not an issue. I'll make sure your rent is paid on time."

"Thank you." Amanda leaned back in her seat, relieved.

That wasn't so bad. Just have to ask for what you want, right?

"Of course. I want you to feel taken care of. You're part of the family now."

"I do, Erica. You've been so wonderful about everything."

Erica smiled. "Believe me, I'm just getting started. It just gets better from here."

They reached the coast after an hour and a half, then Lawrence turned north and drove up Highway 101. The coastline was just as Amanda remembered, a vast expanse of ocean. Waves crashed onto the rocks. Just a few clouds, and the sun shone brightly in the sky. No sign yet of the storm she'd heard was on the way.

She stared out the window in awe. "It's beautiful."

"Aren't you glad you came with us?" Erica asked.

"So glad. I'd forgotten how good it feels to get out of town for a while."

"Vivian knows where to buy a vacation home."

"How well do you know her?"

"It's funny," Erica said. She leaned back in her seat and stretched. Amanda was once again captivated by the curve of her hips, tight against her dress, and glanced away. "I've known about the Obsidian Lounge for a long time. I've been there a few times over the years. But I've never crossed paths with Miss Starr until now. I did a bit of research on her."

"Really?"

Erica laughed. "Of course. Do you think I would enter into a contract with someone before thoroughly vetting them? I always know what I'm getting into. From everything I've heard, Vivian is a brilliant businesswoman. She runs her club right and treats the girls well. She's had some run-ins with the City, especially years ago when people weren't as, how should I say, progressive as they are now."

"I can imagine. That must have been difficult."

"Yes. She fought to keep her club open and made some enemies along the way. Now that she's telling her story, I'm as interested as anyone in what she has to say."

They passed through a few small fishing towns, eventually turning off onto a private road.

All these rich ladies live out in the middle of nowhere. They must really like their privacy.

"Look at this," Erica said. "What a charming area."

Lawrence drove up to a large steel gate, rolled down the window, and pressed a button. "Trent, party of three," he spoke into the speaker.

There was a beep, and the gate lifted.

Really like their privacy.

The grounds stretched for miles, acres of forests and pastures. Vivian's home wasn't as large as Trent Manor, but it was just as impressive.

Lawrence opened the door for Erica while Amanda let herself out. The three of them walked up to the door, and Clara opened it for them. She had tucked her long blonde hair under a pink watch cap and wore a red wool sweater and blue jeans that hugged her curves perfectly.

Well, this weekend just got a lot better. I was hoping I'd see her again.

"Welcome, ladies," she said. "And gentleman," she added, nodding in Lawrence's direction.

He bowed slightly. "Shall I bring the bags in?" he asked.

"Here, let me help you," Amanda said. They walked back to the car together and returned weighted down with luggage.

"Why, Clara," Erica was saying, "I didn't expect to see you here. This is such a pleasant surprise."

"Vivian asked me to help this weekend." She smiled at Amanda. "I love coming out to the coast. It's so peaceful."

Lawrence set Erica's bags down and awaited his next orders.

"I can help bring those in," Clara said. She grabbed one of Erica's suitcases and lugged it inside. "You're just in time for tea," she told them. "Vivian's latest craze is traditional English tea time. You know, crumpets and stuff. I think it's ridiculous, but please don't tell her I said that. And the cookies are to die for."

"Tell me you said what?" Vivian asked. She stood in the hallway in a flowing white dress. She seemed relaxed and comfortable, and Amanda noticed again what an attractive woman she was.

I'll bet she has her choice of women. And is probably an amazing lover.

"I was just telling them about tea-time," Clara said.

Vivian laughed. "Please permit me my indulgences. I have so few anymore."

"Do you need anything else, Miss Erica?" Lawrence spoke up.

"No, I don't believe so."

"Very well. I'll be going, then. Have a wonderful night, ladies. I'll be back in the morning to drive you to the spa." He bowed slightly and walked back to the car.

"Lovely man," Vivian commented. She turned to Clara. "Have you told Amanda about the beach yet?"

"It's lovely," Clara said. "The water's too cold to swim in, of course, but that's what the pool's for. I'll walk you down later and we can watch the sunset. Would you like that?"

"Oh, yes," Amanda said. "I can't wait to see the water. It's been a long time."

"Well, come in, ladies," Vivian said. "Get settled in and freshen up a bit, if you'd like. Tea will be served at four o'clock, just like they do in England. Clara, would you show them to their rooms?"

"Of course," Clara said. She picked up Erica's suitcases. "Please follow me."

Their rooms were across the hall from each other. Clara set the suitcases down and Erica excused herself. She had the larger room, but Amanda's was still more space than she needed.

The bed was king-size, with thick, light blue sheets and far too many pillows. Her room had a gorgeous view of the ocean. A craggy rock jutted out into the sea, and she spied a small lighthouse nearby.

"Is that a real lighthouse, Clara?" Amanda asked.

"It's been abandoned for years," Clara told her. "The Forest Service planned to turn it into a museum, but that never happened. Vivian bought and restored it a few years ago. I'll show you later if you want. It's amazing."

"Sure. That would be great."

Amanda rolled her suitcase into the corner and collapsed on the bed. Clara stood in the doorway, and Amanda felt a gaze up and down her body.

Checking me out, huh? I hope you like what you see.

"I'll call you in twenty minutes," Clara said. "I need to set the tea up."

"Do you want some help?"

"No thanks. There's not much to it. I've got it down." She smiled and turned to leave. "And after tea, we can take that walk. You'll like what I have planned."

"I'll bet I will."

Vivian received them in the front parlor. Three silver platters displayed the fanciest array of cookies Amanda had ever seen. Complex and intricate, lightly dusted with pink and light blue powder, she felt a little bad for eating them. But when she saw Erica take one, she followed suit.

Oh, wow. These are ridiculously good.

Clara poured tea all around and they sat around a table with fancy white linens.

"Where is your housekeeper?" Erica asked. "A house of this size requires a lot of help."

"I sent her away until Monday because I want us to be able to speak freely. I adore Janet, but she doesn't know anything about the Obsidian Lounge, and wants to keep it that way." Vivian lowered her voice to a whisper. "I think she's sexually repressed."

"Well, bring her to the club sometime," Erica said. "One of Sapphire's private dances might bring her out of her shell."

"Oh, she wouldn't like that, and I would never ask. Her role in this house is strictly professional. She prepared a lovely meal for us before she left. It just needs to be heated and served. We can handle that, right, ladies?"

"I'm happy to help out," Amanda said, taking a sip of tea. "Let me know what I can do."

"You're an absolute delight, Amanda," Vivian said. "Thank you. I know you and Clara will work well together."

"Oh, yes," Clara said. "I know my way around this kitchen well pretty good, and it will be even easier with two of us." She gave Amanda another flirtatious smile.

"Well, let's hear about this day trip you have planned for us tomorrow," Erica said. "I hope it's the place I think it is. I apologize, I can't recall the name."

"Oh, you've been to Casa Sirena before?" Vivian looked at her, one perfect eyebrow arched with surprise.

"Casa Sirena!" Erica clapped her hands in delight. "That's it, of course! A lovely place, with the most accommodating staff. I've meant to return for years. Their services were an absolute delight."

"Their services," Vivian repeated dreamily. She straightened up. "Enough talk of that. There will be plenty of time to for us to play tomorrow. Shall I tell you why I asked to spend the weekend here?"

"Yes, please," Erica said.

Vivian took a sip of tea. "I work hard to make the Obsidian a good place. For our customers, and for my staff. A place where women from all over the world can be comfortable to express themselves and explore their sexuality. A place of safety. I take pride in it." She looked at Amanda. "Last night was your first time at my club, I believe."

"Yes," she said.

"How did you like it?"

"It was wonderful, Vivian. I had a great time."

"You enjoyed yourself?"

"Absolutely."

"You felt safe?"

Amanda replayed the private dance with Sapphire in her mind. She tingled just thinking about it, how she'd spontaneously licked Sapphire's nipple, how she'd fingered herself until she'd come on Sapphire's lap.

It was so fucking hot. I can't wait to go back.

"Completely," she answered.

"I love to hear that," Vivian said. "It makes me so happy. That's the way I want my club to be." She paused. "What if I told you the Obsidian Lounge hasn't always been that way?"

"What do you mean?" Erica asked.

"We had an incident at the club a few years ago with a patron. A very famous woman - you'll be shocked if you ever find out who she is. I know I was. She felt that she should be allowed to behave in a way that was not consensual."

Vivian took another sip of tea and held the cup in her hands. Her eyes narrowed. "Completely unacceptable. The employee didn't speak up immediately, and it might well have been forgotten. But she finally did, and I'm so glad for that. I intend to expose what she did, and you're going to help. We'll compile our evidence and present a solid case. There's going to be an explosion when it comes out, I can guarantee that."

"I'm ready to start," Erica said. "Tell me what to do first. I assume you've set up an interview with this employee?"

Vivian sighed. "No. She no longer works for us, and has been difficult to track down, even with all my resources." She set her cup down decisively and changed the subject.

"Time to start dinner, girls. Follow me to the kitchen and I'll show you what to do."

"I hope you like cooking and cleaning," Clara said as Amanda handed her their dirty cups and plates. She quickly stacked them in the dishwasher. "I don't know about you, but that's why Vivian brought me here. She's helpless when it comes to these things."

Amanda set a stack of small plates in the sink. "I don't mind. If Erica hadn't found me, I'd still be at Sam's Clubhouse pouring coffee."

"You were a waitress?"

"Hey, I needed a job," Amanda said. "I have a degree in English but couldn't find work anywhere. Waitressing is a way to pay the bills."

They continued washing dishes, standing close to each other. Clara handed her a plate and their hands touched. They stayed like that for a moment, feeling the energy coming from each other, until Amanda broke it off.

Okay, that was intense. I like where this is heading.

"I get it," Clara said. "I started at the Obsidian as a dancer. It was good money, and I enjoyed it. But when Vivian found out how good I am with numbers, she wanted me in the office." She finished stacking the dishwasher. "It's been a great experience. I've learned a lot, and Vivian is so good to me." She closed the door and turned the knob. "I miss dancing sometimes, though. I miss the connection, you know?"

I'll bet you were fantastic, Clara.

Vivian poked her head in the kitchen. Now that tea-time was over, she held a glass of white wine.

"Erica is going to interview me upstairs. Can you two can entertain yourselves until dinner?"

"I think we can. I'll take her down to the beach."

"Oh, that's wonderful. It's so lovely. Have fun, you two."

"We will." Clara turned and smiled. "Are you ready?"

"You'll need a coat," Clara said as they walked through the parlor. "It gets really windy out there."

All Amanda had was a thin denim jacket. Clara gripped it, subtly brushing her arm, and she felt another tingle.

"No, this won't do at all. You'll freeze. Hang on a minute, I've got something you can wear." Clara looked in the closet and brought out a thick down jacket. "This is better, don't you think? And I think it'll fit you."

Amanda tried it on, and it was perfect. "Thank you."

Clara smoothed the jacket down on Amanda's shoulders, pressing down and rubbing her arms. "Of course. You can thank me again when we're down there."

They walked down the driveway and veered onto a path through the woods. Amanda followed Clara through a grove of giant trees, the salt air rejuvenating her spirit. She felt how close the ocean was and was drawn toward it. They walked together until they reached the beach. The sun inched closer to the horizon as they walked to the edge of the shore and watched the waves roll back into the sea.

"Do you come out here often?" Amanda asked. "I'd be here all the time if I could."

"Every couple of months. Sometimes Vivian comes here by herself, other times she has houseguests. And every so often she brings me along, usually when she's sent Janet away. I don't mind, it's nice to get out of the city." She faced Amanda and took her hands in hers. "What I love most is the privacy. No one's around, and we can be as uninhibited as we want. Like, if we wanted to kiss each other, we could." Her expression was a mix of shyness and lust, and Amanda was momentarily caught off guard by her words.

"You want to kiss me?"

Clara leaned in and kissed her passionately. Amanda responded and wrapped Clara in her arms, letting her hands wander and touch her ass lightly. Clara grabbed her hands and pressed them down hard against her thighs.

"Does that answer your question?"

Amanda nodded. "Yes, but now I have more questions."

Clara pressed herself closer. "Ask away."

"How long have you wanted to kiss me?"

"Oh, girl. I've had my eye on you ever since you walked into the office last night. I was so glad when Vivian said you were coming. This weekend would have been boring without you."

They moved over to a large piece of driftwood, arms around each other, and cuddled close. The wind had picked up, and they nestled next to each other for warmth. Amanda rubbed her hands on Clara's thighs.

"You so feel nice," she said.

"Just wait until I show you the inside of the lighthouse. It's going to blow your mind."

"I can't wait."

"You'll just have to." Clara took Amanda's hand and led her back up the trail to the house.

Janet's dinner was wonderful, and after they had served and cleared and put the dishes away, Amanda lay on the bed in her room reading. There was a knock, and Clara came in and sat down next to her.

"Are you ready for an adventure?" she asked, patting Amanda softly on the butt.

"Did the ladies go to sleep?"

Clara let her hand sit for a moment, then gave a slow rub. Amanda felt the friction and was instantly turned on.

Oh, girl, you're just asking for it tonight.

"They're out like a light. Come on, let's go."

They walked through the woods until they reached the lighthouse. It was old and rundown and looked like it had weathered many harsh winters.

"Doesn't look like much from the outside, does it?"

"Looks like it's been sitting for a long time."

"Well, check this out." She took a plastic card out of her pocket and swiped the door. It opened with a click. "Vivian gave me the key and said we could come down here. She's the only one with access."

Amanda followed her through the door. It was warm inside, and everything was clean and modern. There was a small kitchen and a living room with a couch and a large television. It was the perfect little get-away.

"This is amazing," Amanda said. "Vivian did all this?"

Clara laughed. "I mean, other people did all the work. But she spent a lot of money on it. You haven't even seen the best part. Come on up and I'll show you the master suite."

A spiral staircase in the middle of the room led upstairs. They walked up, and it opened to a large, carpeted bedroom. The king-size bed was covered with a gold and black comforter and half-dozen red pillows. Large windows took up most of one wall and gave a magnificent view of the ocean.

"Vivian turned the upstairs room into a place for receiving her guests, but she never uses it. Such a shame, it just sits here."

She jumped on the bed while Amanda took her shoes off. "Good idea," she said, and started unlacing her long black boots.

"Let me do it," Amanda said. "I'm going to be honest with you. Boots are kind of a kink of mine."

"Is that true? Ooh, I love it." Clara stopped unlacing and waved her leg. "Yeah, why don't you help me out of them?"

Amanda knelt on the floor and took one of Clara's boots in her hands. She pulled it off slowly, savoring the moment. "These are the shoes you can afford when you work for Vivian Starr, I guess," she said.

"Among other things. My salary allows me to do things I never could have imagined before."

Amanda took the other boot off and slid her hands up Clara's legs, which were spread wide.

"For instance, these panties I'm wearing. You wouldn't believe me if I told you how much they cost."

Black and frilly, Amanda swooned at them. "They were worth every penny."

"Feel them, they're so soft. You'll flip."

Amanda rubbed them. "Yes, they are. Delightful." She climbed on the bed and straddled Clara, leaning over and kissing her passionately.

Clara responded by grabbing Amanda's thighs and pulling her in closer. "You're so fucking sexy, Amanda. I'm glad you're here. You make everything about this weekend so much better."

She rubbed Amanda's ass, hands exploring every inch. She started unbuttoning Amanda's shirt. Amanda took it off the rest of the way, then unhooked her bra and threw it on the floor.

Clara leaned in and took one of Amanda's breasts in her mouth. She swirled the nipple with her tongue and grabbed Amanda's other breast, feeling both nipples harden.

"Wow, you're so responsive," Clara said. "Incredible."

"I've always been sensitive that way. It's a curse."

"Or a blessing," Clara said, licking her fingers and sliding them down Amanda's panties. Amanda guided them to her pussy, and Clara rubbed her until she was wet and ready.

"Take them off," Amanda said.

"With pleasure." Clara slid Amanda's panties down and off with both hands. "Are you ready for this?"

Amanda moaned in anticipation. "Oh, yes."

Clara leaned over to kiss the side of Amanda's neck and whispered in her ear. "You can be as loud as you want."

She disappeared between Amanda's legs. Starting with broad strokes of her tongue, she slowly made her way up to Amanda's clit.

"Fuck yes, that's the spot. Right there." Amanda's fingers tangled in Clara's hair as her orgasm built. The wind whipped outside the window and Amanda shuddered in delight as she came hard. She laid on her back and waited for breathing to slow down again.

"Damn, girl. You're amazing."

"I love eating pussy, and yours is delicious."

"Let me return the favor?"

"Oh God, yes. Come over here."

"Lie down and I'll rock your world."

Amanda turned over and pounced on her playmate. "First thing, that shirt has to go."

Clara took her shirt off and exposed her medium-sized breasts. Amanda took one in her mouth and rolled it around as the nipple swelled.

"Wait a minute," Clara said. "You've got to see this. It's the best part of the whole place." She took Amanda by the hand and led her to an old oak armoire. She opened it, and inside was an entire shelf of dildoes and vibrators ranging in size from small bullets to a massive, twelve-inch dong. Another shelf held bottles of lubricants in dozens of colors and flavors.

"Holy shit!" Amanda exclaimed. "What's this treasure chest I've found?"

"Can you believe it? Vivian stocked it up and forgot about it. Never even been used, as far as I know. It's just sitting here. So wrong." She picked up a jar of clear liquid. "This stuff is amazing." She handed it to Amanda. "Expensive, and worth it."

Amanda admired the wide assortment of toys on display. "What's your pleasure?" she asked. "Does anything leap out at you?"

"How about if I let you choose. Just nothing too big, okay?"

"Coward."

Clara laughed and lightly smacked her butt. "Not at all. I'm just realistic."

"If you say so." Amanda eyed a likely candidate, seven inches long and sparkly purple. "That one's pretty, don't you think?"

"Ooh, I love it. Yeah, fuck me with that one."

Clara reached in and picked it out, handed it to Amanda. She led the way back to the bed and laid down. Amanda twisted the cap off the lube and put a few drops on her fingers. She brought them down and traced around Clara's lips. They slid in easily, and she moved up and kissed Clara on the mouth while stroking her.

Clara gasped with pleasure. "You have the magic touch."

Amanda reached for the dildo, expertly applied lube to the end, and spread it around. She slid the dildo in and out as she watched Clara's muscles contract. She leaned in and licked around the edges of Clara's pussy. Bringing the dildo down, she found her clit with her tongue and pressed down hard. Clara's pussy spasmed, and Amanda continued making small circles. She took her lubed finger and gently touched Clara's asshole, rubbing her until she spasmed and her body arched up.

Clara shrieked with delight. "You're so fucking dirty. I love it."

The dildo glided in and out effortlessly as Clara reached another climax. Amanda kept her tongue pushed hard against her clit and rode the orgasm out, Clara's juices covering her mouth. She slid up and kissed her.

"In case you were wondering, you taste delightful."

Amanda woke to Clara shaking her. It was still dark outside, but the storm had passed.

She yawned and rolled over. "What time is it?"

"Still early," Clara said. "But we should get back. The ladies will wake up soon, and we should be there. After all, someone has to make the coffee."

Amanda laughed. "Yeah, I'm sure it's beyond Erica's capabilities."

"And Vivian's. What would they do without us?"

Amanda looked around the bedroom and sighed. "I hate to leave this place. It's so cool."

"Isn't it? I could stay here all weekend with you. We'll come back, I promise. It's waiting anytime we want."

"That's great news," Amanda said. "Now help me look for my bra. I can't remember where I threw it."

Amanda managed to get a few hours of sleep before a soft knock on the door woke her up.

Erica poked her head inside. "It's eight o'clock, time to get up. You must have really needed your rest, Amanda. You didn't stay up too late last night, did you?"

She rolled over and smiled as she remembered her evening with Clara. "Well, maybe a little."

"Oh, to be young again," Erica said. "I, on the other hand, was in bed by ten o'clock." She stood in the doorway, her hand on her hip. "Well, come on. Vivian's treating us to breakfast, then we'll have our day-trip to Casa Sirena. And, really, who am I to argue? I know this is a work trip, but I certainly don't mind."

"You're the boss," said Amanda.

I don't mind, either. This is the best job I've ever had. By far.

"You're going to love this place, Amanda. It has massages, saunas, everything. I've been there once before, and I'll never forget it."

"I'll jump in the shower and be ready in ten minutes."

"Fabulous. See you downstairs."

They sat around the parlor table drinking coffee. Clara had brought out more cookies, and Amanda helped herself.

"Do you mind calling your driver, Erica?" Vivian asked.

"Absolutely. Lawrence is just down the road at a little B&B."

"Wonderful."

All four were dressed casually today. Amanda wore a sweater and jeans. Even Erica seemed slightly less glamorous than her usual self.

"I know we made very little progress on the book," Vivian said. "I apologize for that. But it's so nice to get out of town for a little while. I didn't realize how stressed I've been lately until I got here and slowed down for a minute." She gave Erica a knowing smile.

Ha, I saw that. I wonder what those two were up to last night. I can only imagine, but I'll bet they had a good time.

"No need for apologies, dear," Erica said, giving her leg a soft tap. "This trip has been a delight so far, and you're a marvelous hostess. You've enjoyed our little vacation, haven't you, Amanda?"

"Absolutely." She took another bite of cookie. "I'd come back anytime."

"I should come out here more often," Vivian said. "It's good for me." She turned to Clara. "Remind me I said that the next time I get overwhelmed. Promise?"

"More weekends at the coast," Clara replied. "I'll mark it in my planner."

Lawrence pulled up in the Mercedes fifteen minutes later. He was clean-shaven and seemed well-rested. His chauffeur uniform was crisp and pressed, and it fit him perfectly.

Dapper as always. How does he do it?

"Shall we go?" Vivian asked. "I'm starved. Sending Janet away was a bad idea."

Amanda and Clara shared a secret smile.

"And how did you sleep, Lawrence?" Erica asked.

"Wonderfully. A little rest was just what I needed."

"I'm so glad," Erica said. "You deserve it. You're always so good to me."

"Vacations for everyone!" Vivian said, raising her coffee cup in the air.

Breakfast was amazing, of course. Vivian and Erica had insisted that Lawrence come inside and eat with them, and they all enjoyed the buffet. Servers stood at attention and made their omelets and waffles to order. They all filled their plates and Amanda, at Erica's urging, ordered a second mimosa.

After they had eaten, Lawrence drove them up the coast. The sun had come out and filtered through the car window onto Amanda's arm.

This is awesome. I should really get out more. I need more weekends like this.

"It's just how I remember it," Erica said as they pulled into the parking lot. Casa Sirena sat on a huge parcel and overlooked the ocean. The main building was painted soft blue and white, and there were several small cabins off to the side.

"Those are the guest houses," Vivian told them. "Some people stay for the entire weekend, but I'm sure the afternoon session I've reserved will suit us just fine."

"Unfortunately, you can't come in with us," Erica told Lawrence. "Sorry."

"I know, I know. Ladies only." He laughed. "I'm used to it by now. Believe me, I'll have no problem entertaining myself."

"I wish I knew what you did when you went off by yourself," Erica said. "You never tell me."

"Now, Erica, don't pry," Vivian said. "It isn't polite. If Lawrence wanted you to know what he does on his own time, he'd tell you."

Erica gave a devious smirk. "I'll get it out of him one day. You just watch."

"We'll see about that," Lawrence said, and winked at Amanda.

"A man of mystery," Vivian said. "I love it."

The inside of Casa Sirena was even more magnificent than the outside. The ocean theme continued. Statues of full-breasted mermaids lined the hallway and erotic paintings lined the walls.

"Everything's so sexy here," Amanda said to Clara. "What kind of place is this?"

"It gets better. You just wait."

Vivian made her way up to the counter, and the young woman at the desk greeted her with a smile.

"Welcome back, Miss Starr. Thank you so much for joining us again. Are these your lovely companions?"

"They certainly are, Chelsea. So nice to see you again. Is our room ready?"

"Of course. It's all set up, and your massage therapists are standing by. Just follow me and we'll get you set up."

They followed Chelsea through double doors and down a hallway.

"Your retreat this afternoon is completely private," she explained. "We require all guests to shower before we get started. There are secure lockers for your belongings, and afterward we will provide you with Casa Sirena robes. They're yours to keep, of course."

She led them into a large room with an entire wall of showerheads.

"I hope you're all comfortable showering with each other," she said. "We have communal showers here."

Amanda gave Clara a knowing look.

Very comfortable, I'd say.

"Oh, we are," Vivian said. "We're all close friends here."

"Wonderful," Chelsea said. "After you've showered, dry yourselves off and walk to the next room. Your massage therapists are waiting for you behind that door."

"Isn't this fabulous?" Erica asked Amanda. "Everyone's so nice here." She walked over to the lockers and took her shoes off.

Amanda followed her and began undressing. Vivian and Clara did the same. Soon, all four of them were naked. Amanda chose a showerhead and gently pulled the knob. A soft, warm stream of water fell on her and she sighed with delight.

And it's the perfect temperature. They really know what they're doing here.

She unwrapped a small bar of soap and lathered her arms.

"Amanda, would you mind getting my back?" Erica stood next to her, and Amanda had a hard time not staring at her large breasts and thick, dark bush. "I can't seem to reach. I want to make sure I'm clean all over."

I'll make sure of it. No problem, Erica.

She rubbed more soap on her hands and slowly moved them across the top of Erica's back, building a lather. Erica's skin was soft and yielding, responding well to her touch. She continued to rub up and down, pressing a little harder and inching further down.

Control yourself, girl. Don't get carried away.

"How's that?"

"Oh, thank you." Erica turned and faced her. Amanda hadn't seen Erica's bare breasts since the night she'd spied Sylvie pleasuring her at Trent Manor, and never this close. They were even more spectacular than she remembered, full and heavy, with large nipples.

"Would you like me to do you next?" Erica asked.

An electric thrill coursed through Amanda's body.

Oh, Miss Trent, you have no idea.

"That would be great. Thanks."

She turned around and let Erica's hands slide down her back, rubbing her in soft strokes. Erica put more soap on her hands and brought them down to Amanda's butt. They lingered there for a delicious moment.

"How's that?" Erica asked.

"Perfect. Thank you so much."

"I'm happy to, Amanda."

Erica didn't move her hand. It stayed there, cupping her ass. Amanda leaned in instinctively and Erica subtly ran her finger underneath, brushing her pubic hair.

She knows what she's doing. Damn, she knows I want her.

Amanda leaned back again, a little harder this time, and Erica's finger slid up further, close to her entrance. So close.

Another inch. You're almost there.

Erica brought her hand back up, and Amanda sighed silently in frustration. She turned around to face Erica, who watched their two companions with rapt attention, her hand straying down to her own pussy.

Clara and Vivian stood facing each other, water cascading down their bodies. Clara ran her hands over Vivian's breasts in circles as foam ran down her legs, then smiled and continued washing Vivian's chest.

Erica leaned against the porcelain wall, her hand rubbing between her thighs and over her dark bush. Amanda caught her eye and Erica let her hand slowly move away.

"I feel so clean now, don't you?" Erica smiled and turned the water off.

Their shower over, Amanda dried off with a soft towel and put on one of the white robes. It felt heavenly against her naked skin. After they were all dry, they walked out of the showers and Vivian opened the door. Inside was a room with four more doors. Four massage therapists in matching white uniforms stood at attention.

"You'll love this," Vivian told them. "These women are all experts in the art of massage. Fully accredited and experienced. Go ahead, Amanda, choose your massage therapist."

They all looked great, but she was drawn to one in particular, a young East Indian beauty who seemed open and friendly. She had flawless, light brown skin and expressive, dark brown eyes. Her crisp white uniform fit her compact frame perfectly, and Amanda followed her cute, lean bottom into the room. The lighting was dim and relaxing, and soft flute music played from a speaker on the ceiling.

"My name is Dee," the girl said. "I'll be your massage therapist this afternoon."

"I'm Amanda. It's nice to meet you."

Dee shook her hand. "If you'll have a seat, I just have a few questions to ask you. When is the last time you had a professional massage?"

"Never."

"Really? Well, don't worry about it. I'll take care of you. The first thing I need to know is, do you have any problem areas? Places that need extra attention, or places you'd prefer I keep away from?"

Amanda thought about it. "My neck. I know I keep a lot of tension there. And I guess my arms, too." She sighed. "All over, really."

"Can I ask what you do for work?"

"I'm a - I mean, I was - a server."

"Ah, yes." Dee smiled knowingly. "I spent a few years serving when I moved to the States, before I got my massage license. My arms and shoulders were killing me all the time. Running those plates back and forth all day, it's grueling. So, you don't work in a restaurant anymore?"

"No, I work for Miss Trent, one of the other guests."

"Okay, this is good. Now that I know where I need to focus, you can relax and leave everything to me. I can hang your robe up if you'll get on the table and under the sheet."

"Sure." Amanda took her robe off and handed it to Dee. It felt natural to be naked in front of her, and she took her time getting under the crisp, white sheet. It was nice and cool against her skin, and she sank into the table.

"I'm going to start with you facing down," Dee told her. "Feel free to adjust the face cradle if you need."

Amanda moved her head around. "No, this is good."

"Perfect. I'll start with your neck and shoulders."

Amanda closed her eyes and breathed slowly through her nose. She heard Dee put oil on her hands and rub them together. She started on the back of her neck, and the pressure felt wonderful.

"Wow," Dee said. "So, I can already tell you have quite a few issues."

"What do you mean?"

"Knots. Feel." Dee pressed down on Amanda's neck and it popped. "Right there. Do you feel that?"

Amanda nodded.

"I can get some of them out today, but I would definitely recommend regular massage sessions for you. How long did you work as a waitress?"

"Ever since I got out of high school. About five years."

"I see. Well, just relax, Amanda. I'm going to take good care of you this afternoon." Dee continued to press on her neck and shoulders.

"Ow," Amanda said.

"Too much?"

"No, it's just. Wow."

"It's working, right?" Dee moved her hands over Amanda's shoulders and rubbed them in circles. They both popped. "I told you. This right here. This is where you hold your tension. Way too much tension."

"I know," Amanda said. "I've been stressed out ever since I graduated from college."

"Do you meditate?"

"Why? Do you think I should?"

"At least consider it," Dee said, making her way down Amanda's back. "I find that it helps me a lot. I have a few simple calming techniques I can share with you, if you want."

"Sure."

"For now, let's keep working those knots. That's the first step."

Dee pressed down on her hips. "How's that? Good?"

"Yes."

She made her way down to Amanda's ass cheeks and kneaded them with her hands. "And that? Still good?"

"Mm-hmm."

Dee made her way down even further, first one leg, then the other. She finished by rubbing both her feet down to her toes.

"All right," she said. "Flip over so I can get your other side."

Amanda flipped over onto her back. The sheet still covered her breasts, and she held her arms straight to her sides inside of it.

Dee massaged her neck and collarbone. "Can you move the sheet down a little? I need to get your front."

Amanda reached up with one hand and pulled the sheet down slightly

"Um, little more, please."

"Okay." Amanda pulled it all the way down past her breasts. She felt exposed, but safe. Comfortable. The cool air circulating around the room breezed over her nipples and she smiled.

"That's perfect, thank you."

Dee added more oil to her hands and continued to massage Amanda's neck. She pressed down, passing over Amanda's breasts.

"How is that?" Dee asked.

"Wonderful. I can tell you know what you're doing."

"Thanks. I've been doing this work for five years now, and I've learned a few tricks. I'll teach you a few of them this afternoon."

"That would be great."

Dee walked around to Amanda's feet and rubbed her legs all the way up to her thighs, then back down. She made a couple of passes, each time getting a little closer to Amanda's pussy. Dee's hands were soft yet firm, professional. She touched Amanda's hips, pressing both sides of them, and Amanda moaned involuntarily.

"Did you feel that?" Dee asked.

"I felt something. What was it?"

"I'm breaking up blockages. Have you heard of chi energy?"

"I think so," Amanda said. "Isn't that from kung fu movies?"

Dee laughed. "Sort of. Ancient traditions teach that the body has lines of energy that flow through it. Sometimes they get blocked. There are many reasons for these blockages. Many times, they're stress-related. When I break them up, the energy flows free. You should feel a huge difference in the next few days."

Amanda cocked her head and peered at her.

"I'm serious," Dee said. "This stuff works. Trust me."

"Well, okay. It just sounds kind of woo-woo."

Dee laughed. "It is. It's totally woo-woo. But it works."

Dee kept rubbing until she reached Amanda's inner thighs. Amanda opened them slightly, inviting her in. With each passing stoke, Dee's hands got closer.

"How do you feel, Amanda?"

"Great. You're amazing."

"I'm so glad. I love my work, and clients like you are the best part of the job."

"This is such a treat," Amanda said. "I never do anything like this."

"You deserve to be treated well, Amanda. Do you know that?"

"I guess."

"Well, you do. You deserve all the good things life offers. I can tell you've been working hard for a long time." Dee rubbed closer, achingly, tantalizingly closer to her cunt. So close. "I know you appreciate them. You don't take them for granted like most of the women who come here."

Dee stood in front of her, took her breasts in both hands, and softly squeezed. Waves of pleasure shot down Amanda's body.

"They treat me like a servant. Disposable. I know you're not like that." She traced her finger down Amanda's stomach. "It's rare when a client sees me as an actual human being."

Dee continued her path down to Amanda's pussy. With two fingers, she caressed Amanda's labia, the oil easing her entrance. When she reached Amanda's clit, she softly rubbed in slow strokes.

"Should I keep going?"

Amanda nodded.

Yes. God, yes.

"Good."

Amanda moved her hands to her breasts and rubbed her nipples as Dee increased speed and force, intuitively finding the perfect spot. It felt so natural and right, and the sensations built up quickly. Within seconds, an orgasm began to stir.

Wow, I've never gotten this close so fast before. She's like magic.

"Amanda, can I ask you something?"

"Mm-hmm."

"Do you have any experience with Tantra?"

Amanda tried to think but was too distracted by Dee's fingers. "No, I don't think so."

"I've learned a few techniques that have helped me a lot. I think they could help you, too. Do you want to learn them?"

"I mean, sure."

"Okay. How close are you right now?"

"To coming?"

"Yes."

"That depends."

"On what?"

Amanda laughed. "On you?"

"No," Dee said. "On you." She stopped rubbing, and Amanda let out a sigh of frustration.

"Trust me, this will be enlightening. I'm going to start again. When you get close, let me know and I'll stop."

"But why would you do that?"

"It's part of the training."

"But that's no fun."

Dee brushed Amanda's hair out of her face, caressing her cheek. "Oh, girl. You really don't know, do you? This is going to be great."

Dee started up on Amanda's pussy again. Slow, masterful, strokes.

She's amazing. How does she touch me like this?

Soon she was right at the edge again, so close. Just then, Dee moved her hand away.

"Oh, come on. No fair."

"Not yet. Savor the sensations. Be aware of them."

"I am."

"Not like you can be. I've had orgasms that have lasted over an hour."

"Get out of here."

"I'm serious. You can do it, too. All it takes is practice and intention." She rubbed Amanda's stomach and thighs for a few moments, finally circling back down to her pussy. "I've been having full-body orgasms for the past two years. You feel it everywhere, from the top of your head to the soles of your feet. The first time it happened, it blew my mind."

"I'll bet. How can I have one?"

"I only have time to give you a push in the right direction. There are some great courses, and I'll give you information about them before you leave. For now, just relax and leave it all to me."

Dee poured more oil on her hands and went to work rubbing Amanda's clit. Amanda tensed in anticipation and Dee slowed down again.

"Relax. It's counter-intuitive, I know. Your instinct is to climax, but don't give in to it. Just breathe and be present in your body."

Amanda breathed slowly, in through her nose, out through her mouth. Dee started rubbing again. Within seconds, she was on the edge and ready to go over. She couldn't take another moment and pushed Dee's hand away.

"I can't. If you touch me anymore, I'll come. I can't help myself."

Dee moved up the table and looked down at Amanda. "What if I do this?" She slowly twirled a finger around Amanda's hard nipple.

"Fuck. Fuck yes. So good." Amanda reached out and grabbed hold of Dee's hip. She brushed her hand upward across her thigh, searching.

Dee grabbed her hand. "This is about you this afternoon. Your pleasure."

"And you're just the lowly worker here to cater to my whims?"

Dee smiled. "You're a smart ass, you know that?"

"So I've been told." Amanda dug deeper between Dee's thighs, searching for her treasure. Dee undid her top button and guided Amanda's hand inside. She was hot and wet, ready.

"You know, this was supposed to be a one-way arrangement."

"But?"

"In the interest of excellent customer service, I can make an exception for you."

"Yes, the excellent customer service Casa Sirena is known for. I was told before we got here." Amanda slid off the table and pulled Dee's pants the rest of the way off. She grabbed Dee by the hips and kissed her thighs, then pulled her panties down. She dropped to her knees, slick on the tile floor, and licked deeply as she pushed Dee against the massage table.

Dee pulled her shirt off, revealing small breasts and dark, hard nipples. She rubbed them softly as Amanda continued to pleasure her.

Amanda stood up and faced Dee. "Let me help you with that." She took a breast in her mouth and licked around Dee's nipple as her fingers slid into Dee's pussy and found her clit. She stared into Dee's eyes.

"Are you going to have one of your full body orgasms?"

"I don't think Miss Starr wants to pay for another hour, do you? The Deluxe Package isn't cheap."

"So, you'll come for me?"

"Let me show you."

Dee put her hand over Amanda's and guided her. "Like this. Slow at first."

Amanda continued to stroke as Dee showed her how she wanted to be touched.

"I'm in total control, Amanda. I could come right now, or I could draw this out for hours if we had time. It's up to me. Do you want to learn?"

"Yes."

"It's too bad we don't have more time. The music's going to shut off and lights are going to come on any moment now." Dee moved Amanda's hand away and laid her back down on the massage table.

"I'll make sure you leave satisfied today, but I remember what I told you." She slid her hand between Amanda's thighs and touched her softly. Amanda was immediately back where she had been, on the edge of orgasm.

"Fuck. Fuck."

"Draw it out as long as you want," Dee told her. "You're in control now."

She held on as long as she could. Waves of ecstasy washed over her body and pooled in her wet center until she couldn't take it anymore. She tried to focus on her breathing, to slow down, to remain conscious. But it was too much. Dee was too good. She gave in to her pleasure, orgasms cascading down on each other, and softly sank into the table.

Dee slowly disengaged and put her shirt on as the music faded away and the overhead lights slowly came back on.

"What did I tell you? Right on time."

"Well, I know we didn't get as much work accomplished this weekend as I wanted to," Erica said. "I still hope you enjoyed yourself."

Amber looked out the window and grinned. "I did. Very much."

They had said their goodbyes to Vivian and Clara after dropping them off and loading their suitcases into the car. Now the sun was setting through the trees as Lawrence drove them inland.

"We have our assignments for next week, at least," Erica continued. "Vivian has set up an interview with Sapphire, your dancer from the other night."

Sapphire? That's cool. I'll bet she has some great stories about the club.

"I'm counting on you to take care of this one on your own. I get the feeling I'll have my hands full with Vivian next week."

Yeah, I bet you will.

"I've given your transportation situation some thought, Amanda. I think it will be easier for both of us if you move up to Trent Manor, at least temporarily. It's so inefficient to drive you back and forth to your apartment every day."

"I guess that makes sense," Amanda said.

"Of course it does. Trent Manor has a few guest rooms, so you can have your pick." She clapped her hands together. "Fantastic, then. It's decided. This project won't take more than a month, maybe two."

"What will I do with my apartment in Portland?"

Erica laughed. "Keep it, silly. This is only a temporary arrangement. Besides, it's simple for me to write off your rental costs as a business expense. And you're welcome to return there on weekends if you wish. That is, if we're not traveling."

"In that case, count me in."

"Wonderful. Lawrence will drop you off there tonight. Take care of any business you have and pack what you need for the week. When I get home, I'll have Sylvie send your first direct deposit."

"Thank you, Erica." Amanda smiled as she turned and gazed out the window at the Tillamook Forest.

I can't believe this is my life now. What a difference week makes.

Also by Jasmine Bishop

The Obsidian Lounge
The Obsidian Lounge Episode 1
The Obsidian Lounge Episodes 1-5

www.ingramcontent.com/pod-product-compliance
Lightning Source LLC
Chambersburg PA
CBHW020128180726
47992CB00020B/2545